Sparkle of Glass

by

Shawna Delacorte

Cover Art by *Diana Carlile*

The Wild Rose Press, Inc.
PO Box 708
Adams Basin, NY 14410-0708
Visit us at www.thewildrosepress.com

Publishing History
First Edition, 2024
Trade Paperback ISBN 978-1-5092-5900-7
Digital ISBN 978-1-5092-5901-4

Previously Published Harlequin Silhouette Desire 1995
Published in the United States of America

Chapter One

"Hey, you there—Red!" An angry male shout shattered the morning quiet on the tree-lined main street of Sandy Cove, Oregon.

Darvi Stanton turned her head in the direction of the shout as she closed her car door. Her gaze fell on a tall man with a scraggly beard, shaggy hair, wearing frayed jeans and a faded T-shirt. An unbuttoned, long-sleeved plaid flannel shirt acted as a light-weight jacket.

His stance screamed *confrontation*—one long leg on the pavement and the other on the floorboard of his old, battered pickup truck. She looked around expecting to see someone behind her who would be the target of this disagreeable man's rude shout, but she didn't see anyone.

She turned back toward him. "Are you talking to me?"

"Yeah…you with the red hair. You're in *my* parking place!"

She squinted into the morning sun as she brought her hand to her forehead to shade her eyes. "Since my car is already parked here, I'd say it's my parking space."

"Everyone in town knows that's where I always park."

She glanced up and down the road, then returned her attention to him. "This is public parking on a city street. There isn't any sign indicating parking restrictions."

"Who the hell do you think you are?" His angry question left no doubt in her mind that she had violated his sense of the order of things.

"I *know* who I am." She fixed him with a hard stare, then a condescending smirk that said as much as her words. "Who the hell do you think *you* are?"

Darvi turned her back on him and walked away, but even as she hurried toward her destination, she couldn't dismiss the incident from her mind. She felt his stare bore into the back of her head. She brought her long, copper-colored French braid forward over her shoulder in response to the strange sensation of him possibly coming up behind her and yanking on it like some little kid in grade school.

Foolish thought, but that didn't change the feeling. She suddenly wished she had dressed in something other than the paint spattered sweatshirt and worn jeans, something with a little more dignity and authority. An audible sigh of relief escaped her throat when she arrived at the art supply store, providing an opportunity to get away from the disagreeable stranger, a man who had an oddly unsettling impact on her senses.

"Good morning." She extended a warm smile and offered a friendly greeting to Amy Sutter. Amy and her husband, Frank, owned the art supply store, and Frank also managed the lumber yard next door. "You don't know how relieved I was to get your call about my back ordered paints."

"I can imagine how anxious you must have been. According to my supplier, they were on back order from the manufacturer, which had something to do with importing them into the country. Anyway, I sure was happy when they were delivered this morning." Amy handed her the package.

Darvi paid for the paints, then tucked the box under her arm. "I was beginning to think they were never going to show up. I had a second choice of brand, but I much prefer these." She turned toward the door and called back over her shoulder, giving a smile and a friendly wave. "Thanks for phoning me as soon as they arrived."

Her smile immediately faded when she spotted the same man she had encountered on the street minutes ago now leaning against the doorjamb, his stare fixed on her. She sucked in a calming breath as she brushed past him on her way out the door. As soon as she exited the shop, she came to an abrupt halt. Whirling around, she met his smirking grin.

He raised an eyebrow as he cocked his head and unfolded his arms from across his chest. "You have a problem, Red?" He stood up straight and stuck his hands in his pockets.

She spoke through clenched teeth. "That piece of junk truck of yours is blocking my car. I want you to move it right now."

"You want me to move it right now? I haven't finished my errands yet." His voice dripped with saccharin insincerity. "I'm afraid I won't be able to move it for a while." With that, he turned and casually strolled down the sidewalk toward the lumber yard.

She yelled after him, her frustration overtaking her anger. "Don't you dare turn your back on me. Who do you think you are?"

The stranger turned back toward her, flashed an absolutely dazzling smile that could melt the defenses of the coldest adversary, and mocked her earlier words. "I *know* who I am. Who do you think *you* are?"

****

Darvi pulled her car into the parking lot of the inn located just north of town on a bluff overlooking the ocean. She had always prided herself on her punctuality. The incident from earlier that morning played through her mind, causing her temper to flare. She hated being late for anything. The man in the pickup truck had purposely kept her waiting almost half an hour before letting her out of the parking space.

She looked around the nearly deserted parking area as she climbed out of her car, immediately recognizing the large black car belonging to George Adamson. She had never seen the other vehicle before, a sleek red sports car. When she first met with George, he had described the inn and the type of renovations they would be doing. Then he explained what he wanted from her. She had never seen the interior of the inn or even pictures of its current state.

In addition to being the architect on the renovation project, George also owned the property. She would be providing all the special stained glass windows for the remodeling of the bed-and-breakfast inn, originally built in 1902. He had personally hired her, overruling the contractor's objection and expressed choice of hiring someone else. It was the largest job she had ever been contracted to do, the type of project that could be a real boost to her résumé and guarantee her a successful career. Nervous anxiety tugged at her senses, even though she had full confidence in her capabilities.

As she entered the lobby, she spotted George standing by the fireplace talking with another man whose back was to her. She made her way toward them, offering an apologetic smile. "George...I'm so sorry to be late.

Some scruffy, arrogant jerk blocked me into a parking space this morning with his beat-up old truck and wouldn't let me out. He kept me waiting for half an hour." She turned briefly toward the other man, acknowledging his presence with a friendly smile.

George was a gracious, outgoing man in his early fifties with dark hair graying at the temples. "Don't give it another thought. I just got here myself. Let me introduce you to the contractor on this project. Darvi Stanton this is Rance Coulter. The two of you will be working closely together for the next few months so you need to get acquainted."

Darvi extended her hand to Rance as she carefully looked him over—mid-thirties, dark blond hair, clear blue eyes, and stood about six feet one inch tall. The faint scar starting just below his lower lip extending to his chin presented the only flaw on an otherwise incredibly handsome face. He wore designer jeans and a brightly patterned sweater that complemented his tanned features. There was something familiar about him, something around his eyes and nose, but she couldn't quite place it or where she might have seen him.

"I'm very pleased to meet you, Rance. I'm really looking forward to getting started on this project. It's going to be a real challenge, but I think this will be quite a showplace when it's finished."

Her enthusiasm filled the air, hiding the apprehension building inside her. George had told her the contractor completed several jobs over the last few years with someone in Portland who did stained glass. The contractor had wanted to hire the same man for this job because he knew and trusted the man's work. She needed to put forth her best effort to win his confidence.

Rance felt the soft warmth of her touch as he grasped her outstretched hand in his. He extended the same dazzling smile he had used earlier that day when he had confronted her on the street, not knowing her identity. "Scruffy, arrogant jerk? I'll admit that I certainly needed a shave and a haircut. I'd been tramping around in the wilderness for two weeks, then I spent another two weeks on the beach in Hawaii. I admit my clothes were a mess, although no more so than that *interesting* outfit you were wearing. But...arrogant jerk?"

His voice dripped with sarcasm. "Really, Red—you were the one who stole my parking space. And that *beat-up old truck*, as you so callously referred to it, has great sentimental value to me." He had intended to put her on the defensive with his verbally aggressive manner, a tactic that usually worked to his advantage especially with strangers. It gave him more time to size them up, to categorize them, and determine what tactic to use in dealing with them.

She glared at him, her green eyes flashing defiantly. "Don't call me Red." Then she paused and blatantly scrutinized him. "I didn't recognize you all cleaned up. I'll take back the scruffy part but arrogant and jerk still seem totally applicable."

The smile faded from his face as he stared at her. The realization hit him that he just might have underestimated her. His eyes locked with hers in silent combat. He stretched his tall frame to the maximum.

Darvi Stanton stood a little over five feet seven inches. Tall men did not intimidate her. She refused to back down from his aggressive body language.

George broke the tense moment as he nervously

6

cleared his throat and chuckled self-consciously. "You two seem to have gotten off to a bad start. You're going to have to get along better than this if we're going to complete these renovations on schedule. As you both know, we have a very tight timetable for this project." He stepped between them, placing a hand on each of their shoulders. "Now, why don't you two kiss and make up so we can get on with our business?"

Darvi shot Rance a tempestuous look, then turned her attention to George, giving him her best confidence-inducing smile. "I'm thoroughly professional. I never let my personal feelings interfere with my work." She glared at Rance again. "*My* portion of this project will be completed on schedule and on budget."

Rance cocked his head as he smiled at her. "Are you sure you don't want to kiss and make up? I'm willing to take a chance…for the sake of the project."

Darvi turned an expressionless face to Rance, looked him up and down, then dismissed him with a withering look. Her outward disdain, however, was nothing but a façade. The sensation of his touch as they shook hands had sent tingles across her skin. She didn't like the uncomfortable feelings he stirred in her, an awareness that caused her to be particularly antagonistic toward his comments—more in self-defense than anything else.

Again, George took charge. He stood between them, grabbed both of them by the arm, and guided them through the lobby to the wide curving staircase with the hand-carved banister leading to the second floor. "Come on, let's do a walk-through." Neither Darvi nor Rance said anything.

When they reached the second floor, George

proceeded down the hall. He addressed his comments more to Darvi since Rance had already familiarized himself with the current interior and the architectural drawings for the renovations. "As you know, there will be a total of thirty-four guest accommodations—six rooms on the ground floor, eighteen on the second floor, and six on the third floor—each with a private bath.

"The ground floor rooms have private patios, and the upper-level rooms all have balconies. There are four one-bedroom corner suites—the living dining combination room located on the second floor will include a sofa bed for additional sleeping availability along with a balcony and full bathroom. The suite will extend up to the third floor where the bedroom is located, including another balcony and full bathroom. All rooms will have the availability of connecting doors to the room next door to allow rooms to be combined into a larger area for families or adding a second bedroom and bathroom to the corner suites.

"We have the entrance lobby with its registration area and the dining room where we serve the included full breakfast for registered guests. The dining room will also be opened to the public for dinner, reservations only for a fixed price meal *du jour*. The ground floor guest rooms will be fully handicapped accessible, and in addition, an elevator is being added for access to the second and third floor rooms as part of the renovations. Each room will be decorated in its own dominant color and style. No two rooms will be the same."

They walked through an open door into one of the rooms. "This room is typical as far as size and layout are concerned."

Darvi made notes as George talked, absorbed with

her own concerns and not paying any attention to Rance. She berated herself for having left her good digital camera back at her studio. She wanted to take pictures from each balcony and patio so her windows could relate to the actual view from that room. She temporarily satisfied herself with a few pictures taken with her phone. She would take more extensive pictures later.

They inspected one of the corner suites, then returned to the ground floor and walked outside to the large deck that extended from the back of the lobby to the edge of the bluff overlooking the rocky shoreline. "We'll have afternoon Happy Hour wine and hors d'oeuvres here on the deck for registered guests, weather permitting. Otherwise, it will be moved into the lobby."

Rance eyed Darvi intently as she leaned forward against the railing, watching the ocean waves crash against the rocks below. He silently admitted to a grudging admiration for the way she stood up to his purposeful badgering. Maybe George's insistence on hiring her had not been such a bad idea after all. If her work was half as good as George claimed, this project could turn out to be something very special.

The sunlight caught the copper highlights of her hair. Her smooth, flawless skin emulated creamy silk. She wore very little makeup—a natural beauty, the type that lasted through the years. Something disturbing tried to work its way into his consciousness, but he refused to allow it admittance.

She's stubborn and exasperating. She certainly fits the stereotype of redheads having a fiery temper.

George glanced at his watch. "I have an appointment in Summitville with a client who wants to discuss the design for an office building. I'd better run." He reached into his pocket, withdrew a key, and handed it to Darvi. "Here, take this key to the front door. I'm sure there will be times you'll want to get in when the construction people aren't working." He glanced toward Rance some ten feet away sitting on the deck with his back against the railing.

George returned his attention to Darvi. "I'd like to see some preliminary sketches of the windows, including dimensions and color schemes, in three weeks. Is that okay with both of you? I know it's a tight schedule, but this entire project has a looming deadline that we need to meet."

Darvi shot Rance a quick look, then turned and smiled at George. "I don't have any problem with that." She glared at Rance. "How about you?"

He stood up, dusted off the seat of his jeans with his hands, and smiled solicitously at her. "No problems here."

George shook hands with Darvi and Rance. "Good. We'll meet again three weeks from today, same time. You stay here as long as you need. Just don't forget to lock up when you leave." He hurried out the door and across the parking lot toward his car.

Rance and Darvi cautiously assessed each other. Finally, Darvi broke the silence. "I suppose we'd better exchange phone numbers. It sounds like we'll be seeing a lot of each other over the next few months." She opened her contacts, poised to enter his number, and looked up at him.

He grinned and casually sauntered over to where she stood. "I wondered how long it would be before you wanted my phone number." He reached into his pocket and handed her one of his business cards, showing his office phone and cell phone number.

She turned the card over several times with her long, delicate fingers, then held it up in front of his face. "Don't flatter yourself, buster. This is strictly business." She stuck his card in her large shoulder bag, then pulled out one of her own business cards and handed it to him.

He took a moment to look at it before sticking it in his pocket. "So, they finally rented the Vanowen studio. It's been vacant for six months." He looked her squarely in the eye. "You live in the studio's inclusive apartment?"

Darvi nodded as the words stuck in her throat. Her mouth went dry. His eyes seemed to hold her in his power, exercising some sort of mystical control over her. She found the scent of his after-shave exciting, a realization that left her with an uncomfortable sensation flowing through her body. With great difficulty, she broke eye contact and took a couple of steps back to put more physical distance between them.

Rance pocketed the card, then gazed out over the panoramic scene. He wanted to touch her, to run his fingertips across her cheek. Did her skin feel as silky smooth as it looked? But he restrained himself, refusing to give in to the temptation. "I'll talk to you in a day or two, we can compare notes then. Right now, I have lots to do. As I mentioned, I've been out of town for the last month. Just got back last night."

He flashed one of the dazzling smiles that usually got him what he wanted. "That's how I missed your grand arrival in our fair community…and why you didn't know about my parking space."

At the mention of the parking incident, she visibly stiffened. "You can take your parking space and shove it where—" She abruptly turned and stormed off without bothering to finish her sentence.

He watched with amusement as she walked away. His delight at having gotten the upper hand slowly faded, replaced by a smoldering intensity as he fixed his gaze on her retreating form. He shook his head as he went back inside the building. The job of locking up the inn had fallen to him. After securing the door, he drove home.

Rance owned two acres on the outskirts of town. At the front of the property stood a large, country-style home with an attached three car garage. Behind the house was an over-sized barn that had been converted into a woodworking shop. He pulled his red sports car into the garage next to his old pickup truck, then entered the house from the garage and went immediately to his home office.

Bill Jenkins, his construction foreman, had stopped by periodically during his absence to see that everything was all right. He had stacked four weeks' worth of mail on the desk. Rance settled back in the chair with a sigh of resignation, picked up the first envelope, and opened it. This would probably take just as long as it took him to catch up on his e-mail last night.

****

Darvi fixed herself a quick dinner. As she ate, her mind drifted back to the parking lot at the inn following her most recent confrontation with Rance. She had started her car, then sat there, gripping the steering wheel so tightly her knuckles had turned white as she tried to calm her anger.

What an infuriating man. How dare he talk to me that way. Humph! Insinuating that asking for his phone number in any way implied a personal interest.

What bothered her even more than his arrogant attitude was the attraction she felt toward this totally unacceptable man. With a project that would require all her time and energy, one that had already gotten off to a bad start, she could not afford to be distracted by Rance Coulter. Bottom line—he was the contractor on the job, someone she needed to work with in a cooperative manner. The same man who had wanted to hire someone else to make the stained-glass windows.

A hint of sadness crept over her. She could not afford to be distracted by him—by any man—with or without the added pressure of an important job. Not ever again. Especially not with the devastation and emotional turmoil that had lived inside her every minute of every day for the last two years.

She shook away the disturbing thoughts, went to her studio, and sat down at the worktable. She needed to concentrate on the inn project, not speculate about Rance Coulter. Or worse yet, dredge up her painful past.

Hundreds of ideas whirled in her head. She wanted to get some sketches done while they were still fresh. She did her sketches with colored pencils. When satisfied with what she had drawn, she translated them into watercolor paintings done to scale on heavy white paper. She preferred using watercolors for presentations because they embodied the translucent quality of colored glass. She worked long into the night, totally absorbed in the task at hand.

The clock chimed midnight. She looked up, the late hour catching her by surprise. She yawned, stretched, straightened her work area, and called it a night.

Passing through the sliding pocket door separating

her studio from her bedroom had the feel of stepping back into another century—a time of silky fabrics, lace-edged feather pillows, and gossamer veils. A large, canopied bed occupied the center of the room, covered with a downy soft quilt and pillows. An excellent reproduction of a Tiffany lamp sat on an antique oak nightstand, throwing subdued light across one corner of the room. Tapestries decorated the walls.

A large antique oak dresser rested against the wall at the other end of the room. Numerous framed photographs adorned the top—some old, others recent, and all in antique frames. The bedroom's muted colors of light and dark rose, pale mauve, creamy ivory and beige hues, and various shades of blue suggested a soft sensuality.

The bathroom contained large, fluffy towels in the same muted shades as the bedroom. Scented bath oils and small perfumed soaps in flowered bowls adorned a ledge by the large, claw-foot bathtub. Next to the tub, a modern glass-walled shower.

Darvi quickly undressed and ran a tub of hot water. Her muscles ached from bending over the worktable for so many hours without getting up to stretch. She added some jasmine-scented bath oil, then eased her body into the soothing water. A slight smile of contentment turned the corners of her mouth as her tight muscles relaxed. Then, without warning or invitation, images of Rance Coulter danced through her mind. She quickly opened her eyes. Rance Coulter was definitely not the last thing she wanted on her mind before going to bed.

The next morning, Darvi awoke with a start. As soon as she focused on the clock, she instantly jerked fully awake and threw off the covers. It was late, much later than she wanted it to be. She had intended to be out of bed by six. She missed it by almost two hours.

Darvi pulled into the parking lot of the inn at eight-thirty and immediately spotted Rance's old truck. She grabbed her large shoulder bag, double-checked to make sure she had her camera, and proceeded to the inn where she made her way across the lobby. She shuffled through sawdust and wood chips, sidestepped stacked boards of various lengths, bypassed boxes of tile, and numerous construction tools, none of which had been there yesterday. Sounds of hammering and power saws came from down the hall. Somewhere, a radio blared loud rock music. She marveled at how much the construction crew had accomplished since she left the inn yesterday afternoon. They must have started unloading materials before daylight.

She took photographs on the first floor, capturing the view from each of the rooms and also the common areas of the lobby, dining room, and deck. Then she headed for the staircase and the second floor, relieved that she hadn't seen Rance. As she approached the top of the stairs, he suddenly materialized seemingly from nowhere and stepped in front of her, effectively blocking her path.

Rance studied her. Like the day before when he first encountered her in front of the art supply store, she wore old jeans and a sweatshirt with her long, copper-colored hair pulled back in a French braid. She smelled faintly of some tantalizing fragrance he couldn't quite place. He purposely made an elaborate display of looking at his watch, then shaking his head in a disapproving manner.

"You're late, Red. We've been working for two hours." He caught the quick look of guilt that darted

15

across her face.

"I planned to be here by seven o'clock, but I stayed up too late last night and overslept."

"Oh? And just what is it you were doing that kept you up so late? Some of us are able to handle a social life and still take care of business the next morning." He gleefully noticed the embarrassment his comments caused, but his moment of triumph didn't last long.

"My social life is none of your business." Her eyes flashed her anger. She stepped up to the landing at the top of the stairs, refusing to give him the psychological advantage of towering over her from a higher position. They glared at each other, locked in a silent battle of wills.

Rance brought his other hand out from behind his back and plopped a hard hat on top of her head. "This is a construction zone, Red. Hard hats must be worn at all times. Now, to business. Do you have any information for me yet?" He didn't expect her to have anything ready to share with him but took delight in testing her. "Any hint you might like to give me as to what size your windows are going to be and suggestions on where you think they should be placed?"

Darvi took a deep breath to calm her mounting irritation. She had to make an attempt to get along with this infuriating man. She managed to keep her anger out of her voice. "I asked you not to call me Red."

A mischievous grin played at the corners of his mouth. "So you did…so you did. However, that doesn't answer my question."

"Since it was just yesterday afternoon that we met with George, you can't reasonably expect me to have that type of information for you yet." Darvi adopted a solicitous manner and replied in her most condescending tone of voice. "However, I have completed some of my preliminary sketches."

A quick look of surprise darted across his face, causing a satisfied smile to turn the corners of her mouth. "That's what *I* did last night while you were apparently indulging your social life. Now, if you'll excuse me, I have work to do." Side-stepping him, she walked down the hall to take the rest of her needed photographs.

A hint of guilt poked at her for exaggerating the amount of work she had completed. She had a couple of pencil sketches that satisfied her as far as content, subject matter and color, but she hadn't even started on determining window sizes nor given a thought to possible locations beyond which rooms where those specific windows belonged.

Rance watched as she entered one of the rooms. *She's the most exasperating woman I've ever met. Still, there's something about her…*

He turned and went downstairs, preferring to leave his thought unfinished.

Once satisfied that Bill Jenkins had things under control, he left to take care of personal business. He had done his much-needed laundry last night, but today, he had an empty refrigerator that needed to be replenished. He also needed to talk to Bobby Spencer about helping him with the special woodworking project for the inn renovations.

Bobby was Amy Sutter's nineteen-year-old nephew. He was a wiz at woodworking. He enjoyed helping make the special doors and tabletops with inlaid wood patterns, and Rance was only too happy to pay him for his assistance.

Custom woodwork was Rance's specialty. His father had been a master carpenter and cabinet maker. Rance had learned the skills from him starting at the age of twelve. Even though Rance had a college degree in business administration and a contractor's license, he still enjoyed working with his hands, doing custom woodwork. He had made some furniture pieces, but his favorites were the patterned doors and inlaid tabletops.

As soon as he had heard George's ideas and studied the blueprints for the inn renovations, Rance had pitched the idea of using patterned wooden doors on each of the rooms. Like the stained-glass windows, each door would be different. George had liked the idea, but only if the patterns on the doors related to the patterns in the stained-glass windows so all the specialty touches for each room would be cohesive.

Rance had agreed, but now, he wasn't so sure. It meant he would be working closer with Darvi than he would have otherwise. It also meant her decisions on the stained glass windows would dictate the patterns on his doors. He would be following her choices for this specific portion of the renovations rather than being in charge as the contractor on the project.

****

After Darvi came up with a general idea of the type of scene for the stained glass windows in each of the rooms, she had provided that information to Rance so he could proceed with his door designs. They didn't see each other for three days after that meeting. She worked on refining her preliminary sketches, then started on the more time-consuming work of translating the drawings into watercolor paintings done to scale. First, she figured out window dimensions to accommodate her designs so she could supply Rance and George with the information they needed to adjust the blueprints for construction.

However, the task that presented her with the greatest challenge was keeping her mind on her work rather than dwelling on thoughts of Rance Coulter. Arrogant, antagonistic, infuriating. But at the same time handsome, sexy, and so desirable—at least physically. Certainly not the type of man who would be interested in a committed relationship. But what about a short fling?

Total shock hit her like a thunderbolt. *A short fling?* Where had that come from?

She shook her head in an attempt to dislodge the totally inappropriate notion that had burst into her consciousness—uninvited and unwanted.

Darvi left the art supply store on Saturday afternoon. As she approached her car, she saw a piece of paper stuck under her windshield wiper. She scanned the note. *You're in my parking space again!* Looking around, she spotted Rance leaning against the street signpost, watching her.

He strolled over to where she stood.

"This makes twice, Red." His voice, though soft and intimate, still managed to convey the arrogance she associated with him. "One more time and I might be forced to have your car towed."

A brief moment of serious reflection clouded his features as he reached out and almost touched her cheek. He quickly withdrew his hand.

Confusion ran rampant through her reality. His brief but abrupt change in demeanor almost seemed as if he had permitted a glimpse of a chink in the arrogance he wore like a suit of armor. She quickly shoved away her

confusion and stuffed the note into his shirt pocket.
"Don't you even think about it!"

Chapter Two

For the next few days, they seemed to be constantly running into each other at places outside the construction site—the dry cleaners, drugstore, gas station, and once at a stoplight. Rance was marginally polite, and Darvi was reserved as they exchanged strained greetings. Each encounter left her in a state of quivering confusion. Rance Coulter had an extremely disconcerting effect on her, and she did not like it.

Nor did she understand it.

One afternoon, Darvi struggled with three bags of groceries as she carried them across the parking lot toward her car. A hit of panic jolted her as one of the paper bags almost slipped out of her hands. She tried juggling and shifting the bag, then she lost her grip on the other bags.

"I've got them."

She jumped at the sound of the smooth, masculine voice directly behind her. The grocery bags disappeared from her arms. Turning around, she found herself looking into Rance's face. "Where did you come from?"

Once again, he had her normally controlled manner slightly shaken, leaving her flustered.

"Where did I come from?" He shot her a mischievous grin. "Surely, you must understand that process...the facts of life. But if not, I'll be glad to explain the process for creating a baby. First there's a man and a woman, then—"

"I know the facts of life."

"Sorry, I guess I misunderstood your question. Where did I come from? Well, I was born and raised in Portland, then—"

"You know that's not what I meant." Her words burst out in a flash of anger tempered with just a hint of wariness. "Why were you standing behind me? Are you following me?"

A hint of satisfaction darted through him. "Don't flatter yourself, Red."

The crimson flush of embarrassment colored her cheeks as he used her own words on her. "I didn't mean—"

"You really should have used a cart rather than trying to carry three bags full of…" He looked inside one of the bags containing a carton of eggs and two glass jars. "Breakable things."

"You're right." Her manner softened, in spite of his attempt to rile her. "Thanks for rescuing me. I mean, rescuing my groceries." She reached to take one of the bags from him, but he refused to relinquish it.

"I'd better carry these to make sure they get safely to your car."

When they reached the vehicle, she opened the trunk and stood aside as he loaded the bags. "Thanks."

He smiled as he lightly touched her cheek with his fingertips. "It was my pleasure."

****

The sound of someone entering the room caught Rance's attention, interrupting him as he took measurements in the bathroom of one of the corner suites. Darvi set her large shoulder bag on the floor, then stepped out to the living room balcony.

The remarkably clear day looked as if it belonged on a post card. The sun shone brightly, creating jeweled points of light on the ocean's surface. She closed her eyes and tilted her head back, allowing the warmth of the sun's rays to wash over her face. A contented smile played across her mouth as she slowly ran her tongue over her upper lip. The gentle ocean breeze caught a loose tendril of hair and brushed it against her cheek.

Rance marveled at the texture and quality of her skin, the finely sculpted features of her beautiful face, the curve of her neck, her long delicate fingers resting on the balcony railing. She flicked her tongue across her lip again. He tried to visualize what she would look like with her French braid combed out and her hair flowing over her shoulders.

How can someone that exasperating be so desirable?

He shook his head, unhappy with the thought. He stepped out to the balcony. "Sorry to interrupt your quiet moment of reflection…"

Her eyes popped open as her body jerked to attention. As soon as she focused on Rance, she visibly relaxed and gave him a shy smile. "You startled me. I guess I was daydreaming."

He held her questioning gaze. Questioning what? "I was just going to suggest that we compare notes before proceeding any further."

Something flitted through her eyes, but it disappeared before he could identify it.

A twinge of guilt poked at Darvi. Rance seemed to be proffering an olive branch of sorts, making an attempt to get along. She should have been the one to do that. Yet something about him seemed to constantly attack her defenses, almost as if he purposely went out of his way to antagonize her. She offered a sincere smile. "Sure, that's a good idea. When do you want to do it?"

"I have some business to take care of right now. How about one-thirty this afternoon downstairs in the lobby?"

"That works for me—one-thirty."

As he left the balcony, Rance called over his shoulder. "See you later."

Darvi worked uninterrupted for the rest of the morning, grabbed a quick bite of lunch, and hurried back to the inn in time for her one-thirty meeting with Rance. She waited patiently for fifteen minutes, then nervously paced up and down the lobby, finally glancing at her watch—two o'clock. Rance had her phone number. He could have called, but he didn't.

She leaned back against the fireplace. Irritation over his tardiness built inside her. He couldn't even extend the common courtesy of a phone call. She would give him another fifteen minutes. If he had not shown up by then, she would go to her studio and get back to work.

Fifteen minutes later, she pulled out of the parking lot. Three blocks down the street she spotted Rance standing on a corner, talking with two other men.

He looked up at the sound of screeching tires. Darvi's car came to a halt at the curb. He glanced at his watch. A frown wrinkled his brow as he walked over to her and leaned against the car door. He smiled apologetically. "I was on my way when I got side-tracked. We have a softball game this Saturday and the guys were—"

"You can stay side-tracked for the rest of the day as

far as I'm concerned. I have better things to do than accommodate your total lack of common courtesy and consideration. As I recall, you were the one who picked the time and place, not me. The least you could do is call rather than allowing me to stand there for forty-five minutes waiting for you."

****

Darvi washed and rinsed the last of her dinner dishes and placed them in the drying rack. The sound of the doorbell intruded into her chores. She again thought about asking her landlord to install a dishwasher. Grabbing a towel, she dried her hands on the way to answer the door.

"You're right." Rance flashed his best *please forgive me* smile. "I should have called. I also should have been paying more attention to the time. Mind if I come in?"

She hesitated, deciding whether to shut the door in his face or let him in. After what felt like a very long pause, she finally stepped aside. Regardless of her feelings, they had a project to complete and a tight timetable to consider.

"I really need to finalize those window dimensions."

"Then you should have shown up for our meeting this afternoon."

He seemed oblivious to her comment. "We're almost at a place in the renovations where we won't be able to make any more changes without busting the budget. I also want to compare designs for each of the rooms to make sure your windows and my doors are in agreement. Time is running out. I brought some door samples with me."

Rance held up his carrying case, cocked his head,

raised an eyebrow, and issued a verbal challenge. "I'll show you mine if you show me yours." He caught her wary gaze and immediately assumed a pleasant but definitely businesslike attitude. "We could kick around some ideas if you're not too busy. I want to get Bobby started on cutting the major wood pieces."

"I guess now is as good a time as any." Her smile may have been gracious, but her manner remained cautious and distant. "My sketches are in back."

Darvi started toward her bedroom in the rear of the studio. He followed her. She stepped through the sliding door and pulled it closed behind her, but it didn't completely shut. He pushed the door open and entered the bedroom.

Rance surveyed the surroundings—the muted colors, the soft fabrics, the large, canopied bed. He slowly moved about the room, picking up objects, then setting them back down. He touched the things he could not pick up, felt textures, inhaled the many floral and spicy fragrances.

"I never would have guessed it." He met her gaze. "You're a closet romantic. Under all that anger, tough talk, and defensiveness is this." He gestured with his arm, taking in the entire room. "I'm truly amazed."

He sat on the edge of her bed, bounced up and down, then stood up again. "Nice bed. Feels comfortable." His gaze landed on something silky on top of a lace-trimmed pillow at the head of the bed. His hand closed over a lacy camisole. He looked at her again, the barest hint of a lascivious grin tugging at the corners of his mouth, his very sensual mouth. "No sir...I never would have guessed."

The faint fragrance of roses filled the air. He held up

the delicate camisole by its shoulder straps. "Who would have thought that something like this would be hiding under those faded jeans and paint-spattered sweatshirts of yours."

A shiver darted up her spine as the color of his eyes changed from a clear blue to more of a smoky hue. Anxiety welled inside her, a feeling she immediately shut out with her defense mechanism, the one she used to keep men—those to whom she felt an attraction—from getting too close. A defense mechanism that manifested itself as anger.

"I don't believe there's anything in my bedroom that's any of your business." She snatched the garment out of his hand. "Stop fondling my lingerie."

She glared at him until her anger gave way to embarrassment. They stood very close, their gazes magnetically locked. Only the sound of breathing, both his and hers, intruded upon the stillness of the room. Panic raced through her veins. "Please…wait in the studio. I'll get the completed sketches from my portfolio case and be right out."

A note of caution sounded loud and clear inside Rance's head. He sensed her panic but didn't understand it. What had frightened her? He had categorized her as a tough, in-charge woman, someone who knew the score, could handle whatever came her way, someone who could take care of herself. He had just been presented with a glimpse behind the angry veneer revealing a frightened and vulnerable woman.

"Sure…I'll wait in the studio." He started to say something, then changed his mind. He left the room, sliding the door closed behind him.

He sat on the couch in the living room area of the

studio. It had been a long time since he had been this confused. And his bewilderment came tinged with a healthy dose of guilt. What was it about this woman that seemed to bring out the worst in him? He had actually delighted in trying to determine how far he could push her. He wasn't a disagreeable or confrontational person, at least not under normal circumstances. He had assumed they were evenly matched. She had exhibited every sign of being able to hold her own against his verbal jousting. How could he have misread her so badly? How could he have been so wrong?

He glanced toward her closed bedroom door. She should have returned by now. Was she okay? Should he check on her? He rose from the couch and started toward her bedroom, then changed his mind. Instead, he reached for his carrying case.

Trembling, Darvi sank into the softness of her bed, her sketches in her hand. She gulped in several deep breaths as she tried to calm herself. The look had come into his eyes again, the same one she had seen earlier. A disarming expression that shifted from stunned to intense as if analyzing her through her chosen environment. It was a look that frightened her. Not fear of what he might do but trepidation about the emotions it stirred in her, things she did not want to feel. He had blasted a hole right through her carefully constructed façade without even trying. The wall began to crumble, the wall of protection she had so carefully constructed to hide behind.

She took a calming breath to settle her rattled nerves, then opened her bedroom door. Rance paused from unpacking his case as she walked toward him, his expression questioning.

She returned his gaze, trying to project a casual air. "Is there a problem?"

"No...I guess not." He continued to stare at her, uncertainty covering his face. "Are you all right?"

She glanced down at the floor unable to meet his gaze, then across the room. "Yes, of course. Why wouldn't I—"

He placed his hands tentatively on her shoulders, turning her so she faced him. Shivers of anxiety swept through her body along with a tingle of excitement, the same sensation she experienced when they first shook hands. A moment of relief flashed through her. He had, thankfully, kept her at arm's length.

"Look, I didn't mean to upset you. It was just some harmless teasing..." He lowered his gaze to the floor. "At least, I had intended it as harmless."

The muscles beneath Rance's fingers began to relax, her defenses lowering a little. "It's okay. I...I guess I just overreacted, that's all."

They looked into each other's eyes for a long moment. He dropped his hands from her shoulders and stepped back in a moment of panic. Something about her touched him. He recalled her expression when he had held up the camisole, the vulnerability in her eyes. He felt drawn to her, wanted to protect her, wanted to take care of her...wanted to kiss away whatever fears lurked in the dark, hidden corners of her mind.

He tried to force away the feelings. The last thing he wanted or needed was a relationship, a commitment to someone, or for that matter, to anyone. For him, women fell into one of three categories—business, just friends, or a casual affair—and Darvi didn't strike him as the casual affair type.

Relationships—a vastly overrated concept as far as Rance was concerned. Definitely not for him, at least not anymore. He had been married to Joan for seven disastrous months when he was twenty-three. She ended up running off with the man she had been dating prior to Rance. That had been eleven years ago. He had neither seen her nor heard from her since. He had gotten a divorce and tried to put the entire nightmare behind him, but the emotional scars still ran deep. Since that time, his choice of women had tended toward those with the same *no strings attached* philosophy as his. If he suspected a woman of husband-hunting, that put an end to any further personal association.

Rance turned back toward his patterns and wood samples. "Let's see if we can get some work done before it gets too late."

Darvi allowed an inner sigh of relief, grateful he had removed his hands from her shoulders and turned the moment back to business. Until a little less than two weeks ago, she had no idea Rance Coulter even existed. Now, he caused her to feel things she didn't want to feel. Unanswered stirrings forced themselves into her consciousness. She tried to shake off the awkwardness of the moment and adopt an upbeat attitude.

"Would you like something to drink? I have coffee, iced tea…"

A tentative grin tugged at the corners of his mouth. "I don't suppose you'd have a cold beer handy, would you?"

"I do if you're not picky about the brand." She started toward the kitchen as she continued to talk. "Amy was over last week. She drinks beer, so I bought a six-pack. There are four bottles left." She returned with an opened bottle and handed it to him. "Would you like a glass?"

"No, this is fine. Thanks." He took a swallow from the bottle then gestured toward her empty hands. "You don't drink beer?"

She scrunched up her nose and made a face indicating her distaste, then started laughing. "No, I never acquired a taste for it. I'm more of a wine person."

"I like wine, too, usually with dinner. It's nice to know we have something in common," a wry grin played across his lips, "other than my parking space." Her anger started to flash, but she quickly shoved it aside. His expression turned serious. "It's also nice to see you smile, to see you're not always so uptight, angry, and defensive."

A heated flush came to her cheeks as a shy smile curled the corners of her mouth. "Well, it's nice to see that you aren't always an insufferable, arrogant jerk."

He reached out and brushed an errant tendril of hair from her cheek. His fingertips lingered. Their gazes locked. An eerie stillness filled the air.

Darvi's heart pounded. Blood rushed in her ears. Her mouth and throat went dry as she tried to swallow. Tremors started deep inside, then quickly spread through her body. His eyes turned a smoky blue. He slowly leaned his face into hers, his gaze fixed on her mouth.

She hesitated for a brief moment, then pulled back from him. "I think we'd better get to work before the evening is gone."

He looked at her questioningly, then assumed a businesslike attitude. "I think you're right. My primary concern at this time is dimensions and placement rather than design and color."

"Could we talk color and design for a minute first? The dimensions I have right now won't mean anything if I have to redo designs. New designs will probably change the size and shape of the windows."

"You're planning on windows that don't fit standard sizes and shapes?"

"Let me show you what I have, then you can tell me if it will work."

He looked at her for a moment as he took another swallow of his beer. "All right, that makes sense. What have you got?"

Darvi spread out sketches across her worktable, some still line drawings, others transferred to watercolor. "I want to stay away from bright blue, bright green, and bright red. I don't want this to look like the windows in some sixteenth-century European cathedral. I want to do something modern, yet reminiscent of the softness and sensuality of a time gone by, paying homage to the Victorian era that influenced the design of the original inn's construction. I want muted colors—nothing that will keep anyone awake at night."

"That's incredible. That's exactly what I was thinking—soft colors with a Victorian feel."

"I want the windows to be representative of the view from the room through the sliding glass doors. The ocean-view rooms will depict ocean scenes and the mountain-view rooms will have mountain and forest scenes. I'm going to limit the designs to the same four basic colors. Rooms will have different dominant colors, yet combine all four colors. That way the various colors of sheets, towels, and things like that can be switched from room to room without interrupting the overall flow."

Rance slowly nodded his approval. "I had my doubts last week. I even had my doubts this morning, but I think your ideas and mine will work together just fine."

His gaze captured hers for a brief moment and caught the glow in the depth of her eyes, the enthusiasm she felt for her work. He picked up a couple of her sketches, a slight frown wrinkling his brow. "Some of these windows are unusual shapes and sizes." He held up a triangular-shaped design and another one depicting a narrow vertical oval. "I didn't realize you were planning on using irregular sizes and odd geometric shapes, at least what could be considered odd for the room windows of an inn, rather than standard vertical and horizontal rectangular shapes."

"Is what I've chosen going to really be a problem?" She showed genuine concern. "I guess I was only looking at it from my creative point-of-view. I hadn't considered your practical aspect. Maybe..." She hesitated, not sure how much to compromise her creativity. "Maybe I could try to fit the designs into a more conventional shape and size."

"No..." He studied more of her drawings. "No, I think we'll be okay. The way you've done this will enhance the room much more than the traditional rectangular shape whether horizontal or vertical." He looked up from the drawings, capturing her gaze. "However, this does mean you'll need to firm up your specifications immediately, so I can get the necessary changes to George so he can revise the blueprints. I'll also need to adjust some of my patterns for the doors to coincide with the geometric shapes you've chosen."

"Could I see some of your door ideas?"

He pulled out some patterns, photographs of

previous projects, and wood samples.

Darvi studied the pictures, then picked up a presentation piece he had mounted on plywood. It was heavy, but she was accustomed to working with heavy glass windows and had no trouble propping it up against the wall. The tabletop design used five different types of wood inlaid in an intricate pattern and polished to a smooth finish."

"This is beautiful." Her voice conveyed her surprise. "Do you produce this type of custom woodwork all the time?"

"Not as often as I'd like."

She returned her attention to the design sample, running her fingers across the smooth surface of the wood. "I'm very impressed."

"Thank you." His voice took on a softness, then he quickly regained his business attitude. "I didn't bring any of the construction blueprints with me, so why don't we call it a night and meet at the inn early tomorrow morning? We can do a walk-through and mark the exact location you want each window installed and make sure it works with the structural requirements of the building." He rose from his chair, stretched his tall frame, and downed the last swallow of beer before gathering his materials.

Darvi stood up, too. "That sounds good. Unfortunately, I don't have all the sizes and shapes set yet, but I don't want to hold you up. As far as the other windows are concerned, we can go ahead and determine size and shape so George can adjust the blueprints. I'll design something that will fit. Shall we meet in the morning about seven o'clock?"

"Perfect. See you then." He looked into her eyes.

The panic and anxiety had disappeared, but nervousness and uncertainty still lingered. His gaze dropped to her mouth. He wanted to calm that nervousness, to kiss away her uncertainty.

He sucked in a steadying breath. He wanted to get the hell out of her studio before he tried, once again, to do just that. "Good night, Darvi."

"Good night." Darvi closed and locked the studio door, turned out the studio light, and walked toward the light in her bedroom.

She closed the bedroom door behind her and leaned against it as she surveyed the room. She loved this room. She had decorated it exactly the same as her bedroom in her oceanfront studio in Laguna Beach. When she made the decision to move from Southern California to Sandy Cove, Oregon, her one priority had been to find a studio that included the same type of living arrangement. She couldn't stop the angry frown from contorting her features. And tonight, this room—her sanctuary—had been invaded. How dare that insensitive, selfish, lying, loathsome—

She froze in horror at the realization it wasn't Rance Coulter she had just described. It had been *Jerry Peterson.* A hard shudder shot through her body at the mere thought of him. Her stomach churned. She felt physically ill. Darvi wanted nothing more from life than to permanently erase the despicable Jerry Peterson from her memory.

****

Darvi awoke with a start, sitting bolt upright in her bed, the recurring nightmare lingering. Beads of perspiration dotted her face. Her labored breathing accompanied her pounding heart. She still wore the clothes from the night before. The clock in the other room chimed five times. She reluctantly climbed out of bed and trudged into the bathroom. She took a hot bath, dressed, then gathered her work materials.

At five minutes before seven, Darvi pulled into the parking lot of the inn. She spotted Rance's truck along with the vehicles belonging to some of the construction crew. She grabbed her large shoulder bag and headed for the door.

As she crossed the lobby, Rance called to her from the deck. "Out here."

She stepped through the opened French doors. An involuntary smile spread across her face and warmth surrounded her words. "How delightful!"

He had taken one of the discarded doors and set it up on two sawhorses to make a table. He had set out a large container of steaming coffee, two mugs, and a paper sack containing fresh croissants, still warm from the bakery. Two crates served as chairs.

He returned her smile. "I hope you take your coffee black. I didn't think to bring any cream or sugar."

"Black is perfect, thank you." She sat down on one of the crates. "What made you think of this?"

"It was nothing special." He poured hot coffee into the mugs and set one in front of her. "Just my own natural creative brilliance."

Darvi took a sip of her coffee, not at all sure if his comments were said in jest or seriously. She decided, for the sake of peaceful coexistence, to treat the remark as a joke. "I'll give you points for this one."

Rance captured a moment of eye contact. He searched the depths of her green eyes, trying to see beyond the wall she placed between herself and the rest of the world, not sure exactly what he felt other than something different, something special. He found Darvi Stanton to be an enigma—on the surface hot tempered, exasperating, and frustrating. It seemed they had spent most of their time together clashing over something.

Or more accurately, clashing over *everything*.

Yet he sensed a different person underneath—a vulnerable woman, yet one with an undeniable sensuality. A woman who had chosen to hide behind a façade just as her bedroom hidden behind the sliding door provided her with a sensual retreat so different from her all business studio and the rest of her living quarters. Just what could be so painful that she would choose to hide behind such a tough exterior?

He pulled the other crate next to her and sat down so he wasn't towering over her. "Darvi…what's wrong?" His gaze traveled across her face then settled on her eyes again. She squirmed uncomfortably. "What frightens you so much? What are you hiding from that makes you so constantly defensive and fearful?"

Shock then fear flickered through her eyes before she turned her face away. Her gaze darted across the panoramic ocean scene, nervously seeking out something. What, he didn't know. The silence surrounding them grew louder and louder, until it had completely engulfed them to the point where it even shut out the sounds of hammers and saws coming from inside the building.

He reached out, placed his fingertips under her chin, turned her face toward him, and lifted until he could look into her eyes. He studied her for a moment, then spoke softly. "I'm a good listener. Really, I am, in spite of what you might think."

He offered a sincere smile of encouragement. Her face mirrored the indecision and confusion going on inside her and reflected it in her eyes. It seemed to him that she had been carrying a terrible burden for much too long. She appeared to be on the verge of opening up, then suddenly everything changed.

Her defensive wall shot up again, and she handed him a brusque retort. "What is this, Psychology 101? Do you write a paper and turn it in at the end of the week? For your information, nothing's bothering me. I'm just fine."

She tried to glare at him but without any success. Unable to hold his gaze, she turned away but not before he glimpsed the pain in her eyes.

He sat silently for a moment then abruptly stood. "My mistake." He picked up the bakery sack and held it out to her. "Here, have one of these croissants. The bakery on Main Street makes them fresh every morning. They're very good."

Darvi glanced at the sack, then at Rance. She helped herself to one of the rolls. "They do look good." She gazed at the ground as guilt stabbed at her. "I didn't mean to snap at you like that." She drank the last swallow of her coffee. "I guess I'm a little tired. I didn't have a very good night's sleep." She held up her empty mug and forced a smile in an attempt to smooth over her outburst. "I'll take a refill if there's some left."

"There's plenty."

They sat in silence as they finished their coffee and croissants. Rance threw the napkins and empty paper bag into the large trash receptacle. He picked up the coffee container and mugs, paused briefly, then sat down on the sawhorse. "My offer still holds. I'm a good listener."

Darvi eyed him for a long moment before she looked away. "We should get to work. This is business, remember?"

He stood up, his manner brisk and his words clipped. "Right you are. This is business."

Chapter Three

Rance checked his watch, then studied Darvi for a moment. "It's five-thirty. The construction crew went home an hour ago. What do you say we call it a day?" He started gathering up blueprints, sketches, and the numerous notes he had made during the day. "I don't know about you, but I'm starved. We worked right through lunch." His voice didn't have the confidence he wanted, sounding more tentative than anything else. "Would you like to get something to eat?"

"I don't know…"

Uncertainty clouded her eyes. "For crying out loud, Red. I'm only talking about grabbing a bite to eat. I'm not asking you to be the mother of my children." The words had come out of his mouth before he could stop them.

"I told you not to call me Red. I don't want to have to tell you again." She glared at him for what seemed like eternity before she finally looked away.

He took a steadying breath and carefully measured his words. "I'll tell you what. Why don't we think of it as two business associates having a business meal together."

The direction of the conversation left Darvi uncertain. *The mother of my children* represented the last words she wanted to hear from anyone, least of all Rance Coulter. "I…I suppose that would be all right."

He tilted his head and looked at her questioningly. "Your enthusiasm is overwhelming. Should I have my attorney call your attorney to establish the parameters of what constitutes a business meal so neither of us inadvertently violates the *rules*? I'll let you pay for your own dinner if that will make it more acceptable for you."

She emitted a sigh. "I didn't mean to sound like that." A smile turned the corners of her mouth, half forced and half shy. "Having a business meal with a business associate sounds like a good idea."

"Then it's settled." He finished putting his papers into his case, then they walked outside together. "I want to go home first and wash off the sawdust. Do you want to meet me at the Wine Bistro at seven o'clock?" He paused then cautiously added, "Or would you prefer that I pick you up at your place?"

She hesitated a moment as she turned the idea over in her mind. "I'll just meet you there—that would be better…uh, easier."

Having Rance pick her up at her place was not the problem. What Darvi wanted to avoid was an awkward situation when he took her home. She felt crowded. He had been pressing her too hard, trying to pry into her personal life. The previous night he had even started to kiss her. Or at least she thought he had intended to kiss her. She wanted to do this job. It would be very important to her career and her resumé. She wanted Rance Coulter to stay out of her personal life and most certainly out of her thoughts and dreams.

What she refused to admit, did not want to face, was her desire for exactly the opposite. For Rance Coulter to be an important part of her personal life.

"I'll see you at seven o'clock." Rance headed for the

parking lot as he called back to her. "And try to be on time, Red. Okay?"

She shouted at him, her anger again flaring in response to his words. "I'm not the one who has a problem with punctuality!" She gave it all the volume she could. "And don't call me *Red*!"

He climbed into his truck and drove off.

Humph! The arrogance of the man is unbelievable. I don't even know why I agreed to this.

A wave of guilt hit her. He had only been teasing her, purposely seeing if he could get a rise out of her. And she had taken the bait. Deep down inside, she knew exactly why she had reacted to his comment that way. She had been drawn to him like a moth to the flame and desperately wanted it not to be so.

****

Following dinner, Rance escorted Darvi across the street from the Wine Bistro to the Seaside Art Gallery. The gallery remained open late that evening for a special showing of the latest works of a famous painter who had gotten his start as a local artist. The exhibition had attracted a good crowd, and the champagne seemed to flow nonstop.

Rance watched Darvi as she studied one of the paintings. She wore silk slacks and top, an emerald-green color that exactly matched her eyes. A delicate gold chain adorned her neck, and on her wrist, she wore a matching gold bracelet. Her long, copper tresses were pulled back in what he had come to expect as her trademark French braid.

He took two glasses from the tray proffered by the waiter and handed one to her. "I snagged us a couple of glasses of champagne."

She smiled politely as she accepted the glass. "Thank you."

Again, he allowed a quick fantasy of what she would look like with her hair combed out, flowing over her shoulders or possibly fanned out across a pillow as she…

He refused to complete the thought. "Are you familiar with this artist? He's our *local boy made good*. He's had several showings of his work in prestigious galleries in New York, Chicago, Los Angeles, San Francisco, and also in Europe."

"I saw one of his exhibitions in Los Angeles…very impressive."

"I was fortunate enough to be able to buy one of his paintings when he was still a local artist, before he hit it big. I can't afford him now. It's a seascape. I have it in my home office."

They made their way around the gallery, inspecting each painting. He tried to engage her in conversation. "This is quite an impressive grouping of paintings. I didn't realize he worked in such a variety of subjects."

"Yes, it's very nice. He's an impressive artist." She turned their conversation to focus on work. "How are you coming with the renovations? Are you on schedule?

"Oh, yes…we're definitely on schedule. In fact, in some areas, we are a little ahead of schedule. Things are moving along very smoothly."

"That's nice."

"How are your windows coming along? Will you have a few of them finished sometime soon so we can install them in at least one room to see the overall feel for the finished look?"

"I hope so."

"I know you're new to Sandy Cove. Are you also

new to Oregon?"

"Yes."

A wary, uncertain look came into her eyes every time he tried to talk to her about anything personal. He was beginning to grow frustrated with her minimal answers and no real conversation. "Where are you from?"

"I moved here from Laguna Beach, California."

"Really?" He offered a friendly smile. "Why would you want to abandon sunny Southern California, trade it for rainy Oregon?"

"Oh…California has become way too crowded and much too expensive."

He had noticed all the photographs in her bedroom. Perhaps family would be a safe topic of conversation, one she would be willing to pursue. "Do you have family in Oregon? Perhaps in Portland or Salem?"

"No." She glanced around the gallery as if trying to find something then changed the subject without elaborating on her one word answer. "It looks like they have a nice turnout for this exhibition."

His frustration grew. What started as simple curiosity had evolved into a genuine need, almost an obsession, to know something about her. At this point, to know *anything* about her. What happened in her life to cause so much anger? To make her so defensive? To have hurt her so badly?

He grabbed her hand and led her toward the back door. "It's very warm in here, probably from all the people. Let's step outside and get some fresh air."

Darvi took in a deep breath as they stepped out onto the patio, then slowly exhaled. Rance pulled her into his arms, startling her with his totally unexpected action.

The silvery shimmer from the full moon highlighted his handsome features. He held her close, but not too close. A tremor shot through her body. His after-shave tickled her senses, his touch much too inviting. Her carefully constructed façade began to crumble.

For a brief moment, she did not care. Darvi melted into his arms as he drew her closer, holding her against the hardness of his taut body. It had been a long time—two years to be exact—since she had allowed this type of closeness, to experience the sensations that coursed through her at that moment. He excited her senses, made her blood race. Being in his arms felt good. She didn't want to leave. She rested her head against his shoulder and closed her eyes. For a stilled moment in time, she allowed herself to become part of him, to feel things she didn't want to feel. Things that frightened her.

Then she regained her momentary loss of senses. She quickly pulled away from his embrace. A combination of excitement and panic raced through her body.

"I...It's late. I believe I've had enough fresh air." The huskiness in her voice betrayed the reality she desperately tried to hide. In spite of the cool air, her face felt hot. The smoky blue change came into his eyes as they held each other's gaze.

"I believe you're right. It's probably time to call it a night." A touch of huskiness invaded his voice, too.

Rance felt the tension drain from her body as if she had decided to stop fighting their attraction. It so surprised him that he had almost stumbled backward a step. She had felt soft and warm in his arms with the firm fullness of her breasts pressed against his chest.

An image of her silky camisole flashed through his

45

mind. The insistent whisper of the ocean waves in the background together with the light scent of her perfume penetrated his already overstimulated senses. In a totally impulsive gesture, he wrapped his arms around her again and captured her mouth. What started as a simple kiss quickly escalated. He felt her passion as she responded to his kiss, but it lasted only a moment before she jerked back from him.

"What do you think you're doing?" Her angry words also carried her uncertainty.

"Well, if you don't know I must be doing it wrong." An involuntary hint of sarcasm laced his retort.

"You know what I mean."

Rance leaned back against the wall and studied her a moment. "I was kissing you. I thought you wanted me to kiss you." He took a calming breath. "At least I know it's what I wanted to do."

She pushed past him. "If I want you to kiss me, I'll let you know."

She stormed through the art gallery and out the front door. He had not meant for it to happen that way. He let the cool ocean breeze soothe his confusion and his frustration. Could he have been that wrong? Did he misread her body language that badly? He didn't think so. He'd felt her heated response before she suddenly retreated behind her defensive barricade.

He allowed a sigh of resignation then drove home and went to bed.

But sleep eluded Rance as he thought about Darvi Stanton. One moment nestled warmly in his arms, her head resting tenderly on his shoulder. The next moment hurling her anger at him. He was accustomed to having his pick of women without having to put up with all the clutter. That was the way he wanted it—no promises, no commitments. He wondered if Darvi was really worth all the trouble it would take to break through that wall she hid behind, to find the real woman buried inside. Did someone truly special even live behind that defiance and anger?

Brief images of Darvi flashed through his mind— her dazzling smile when George introduced them before she realized they had already engaged in a confrontation that morning, the great enthusiasm and dedication she showed for her work. Then there was that frightened, uncertain look in her eyes when he had teased her in her bedroom, the soft warmth of her body nestled in his arms, and the momentary spark of fiery passion as she briefly responded to his kiss.

Someone very special lived behind that wall, someone worth knowing. If only he could figure out how to coax that real woman into the open. He finally fell asleep, delectable yet disturbing thoughts of Darvi Stanton filling his dreams.

****

Darvi sat in her car in her driveway for what seemed like the longest time. Tears rolled down her cheeks as she tried to control her emotions. Rance's kiss had stirred something deep inside her. She wanted to respond, had started to respond to his kiss and her desires. Then her fears took over, and she slammed the door shut, protecting her vulnerability and fragile emotions, once again hiding behind the safely of her emotional barricade.

She reeled from the inner battle that raged between her desire for Rance Coulter and her fear of how and what he made her feel. A bigger all-consuming fear

47

questioned how he would feel about her if he ever found out the dark secret of her past. Did she dare take that chance?

She went inside, immediately going to bed. But falling asleep didn't come easily. She tossed and turned for what seemed like forever before managing to doze off. After spending a restless night, she gave up trying to sleep.

Darvi stayed in bed the next morning. More than simply tired, exhaustion claimed her as if she had been doing heavy physical labor for many hours. Rance's kiss had caught her totally by surprise. She had not been prepared for it. Her fingers moved slowly across her lips as the memory of the kiss flooded her reality—his lips soft, his mouth sensual. He had simply set her soul on fire in a matter of seconds.

She closed her eyes and visualized his commanding presence as they stood on the deck at the art gallery, his handsome features bathed in the silvery glow of the full moon. Her eyes popped open. She shook her head to clear it of the image as she stared up at the canopy of flowered material above her head. A sigh, then she forced herself out of bed.

She showered and dressed. As she pulled the last stroke of her brush through her hair, the phone rang. "Amy! This is a surprise. Did I forget to pay for something?"

Amy laughed in her typical outgoing, good-natured way. "No, don't be silly. Nothing like that. It's the start of local softball season. The first game is this afternoon at one o'clock. Since you're new to Sandy Cove, I didn't know if you understood that everyone's invited. Frank's going to be playing. Would you like to watch the game with me?"

Darvi crinkled her nose and furrowed her brow. "Softball? Sounds like fun. I'd love to." And it sounded like a good opportunity to meet more people, to become more acclimated and comfortable with her new town.

"Good. We'll pick you up at noon. We always have a picnic after the game. Think you could make potato salad for about a dozen people?"

Darvi felt her eyes grow wide. "A dozen people?" She glanced at the clock. "By noon?"

Amy's enthusiasm waned a bit. "Is there something you'd rather bring? I can do the potato salad."

Darvi quickly recovered her composure. "No, don't be silly. Potato salad it is. I'll see you at noon." She glanced at the clock again as she hung up the phone. Potato salad for a dozen people? She grabbed her purse and headed to the grocery store.

She stood in the deli section for a few minutes debating whether to buy potato salad instead of purchasing the ingredients. After considering how much time it would take to make potato salad for that many people, she opted for the deli. She rushed home, transferred the cartons of potato salad to a large bowl with a lid, located a large serving spoon, then hurried to get ready for the day's activities.

Amy, Frank, and Bobby stopped by at noon to pick her up. The four of them drove to the park. Darvi scanned the softball field, noting several players tossing the ball and participating in batting practice. She recognized most of them, even though she had never actually been introduced. Some of the players belonged to the construction crew working at the inn.

Then she spotted Rance's red sports car pulling into

the parking lot on the other side of the field. She watched him extract his tall frame from the car, walk around to the passenger side, open the door, and stand aside as a very young and very pretty blonde stepped out. Several men on the field called to Rance. He waved a friendly greeting.

Amy's face became animated when she saw them. "There's Rance and Staci. They'll be joining us for lunch after the game." Amy turned toward Darvi with a bit of background information on the day's event. "Rance is the one who organizes the softball games. He's been doing it for ten years now."

Darvi answered absently. "That's nice." She eyed Staci. *She can't be over nineteen at most. What's he doing with someone that young?*

Darvi continued to watch, aware of her growing irritation at seeing him with another woman and not at all happy about her reaction to the situation.

Well, everyone seems to know her. I guess he must date her regularly. What could they possibly have in common? Humph! Now, that's a pretty stupid question. They probably spend all their time in bed. But if he's dating someone regularly, why did he kiss me? Just a game? Seeing how far he could get?

A hard knot tightened in her stomach. She had seen the two of them arrive in his car and immediately projected an entire scenario based on…on what? And why? Could she possibly be jealous? The spontaneous thought shocked her. The heat of embarrassment quickly spread across her cheeks. Such a ridiculous thought.

She noticed Bobby staring at Staci like a lovesick puppy. *Bobby should be dating her, not Rance. Well, it's none of my business if he dates a mere child.*

Again, she felt a twinge of guilt at her sarcasm. After all, what possible difference could his dating habits make to her? In spite of the kiss, their relationship was strictly business. And barely that.

The game started with a flourish, distracting Darvi from her thoughts. Everyone enjoyed a grand time. The onlookers in the bleachers cheered their team, the players obviously competitive but having great fun. Rance played first base. Darvi carefully scrutinized him. He wore shorts and the team T-shirt. His legs were long, athletic, and tanned. She recalled him saying he had just returned from Hawaii.

The T-shirt accentuated his broad shoulders, strong arms, and muscular chest. She silently acknowledged the tingle of excitement she felt at the sight of his well-toned body. She looked to the other side of the bleachers at the young woman who had accompanied Rance. She, too, appeared quite tan. Tension built in her body, shoving at all her trigger points. Had they shared the two weeks in Hawaii?

She once again dismissed the ridiculous notion that she might be jealous. What an absolutely absurd concept. Jealous? Of what? She shoved the entire theory aside and returned her attention to the action on the field. Unfortunately, in spite of her intentions, the theory continued to poke at her.

The game ended triumphantly for the home team. They won handily, with Rance clearly the outstanding player. He hit two home runs and executed a crowd-pleasing double play, tagging the batter out at first and getting the ball to second base in time to tag that runner.

Darvi's stomach knotted as Staci ran out of the stands, threw her arms around Rance, and gave him a big

51

hug as he came off the field. They hurried toward the picnic table, Frank and Bobby close on their heels. She helped Amy set out the rest of the food.

"Amy, love, everything looks great. I'm starved." Frank reached for an olive and a couple of carrot sticks as he turned toward Rance. "Hey, buddy. Where's the beer?"

"The cooler's in my car. I'll get it."

"Need any help?"

"I can handle it. Be right back." Rance loped across the softball field at an easy gait.

Amy held her hand out toward Staci who stood alone at the other end of the long picnic table. "Staci, dear, come here and meet Darvi."

Staci smiled and walked over. Up close, Darvi could see Staci's perfect features and big blue eyes. Her tanned skin perfectly complemented her long blonde hair. She was even younger than Darvi had first thought—no more than seventeen. Everyone seemed to know Staci and like her. Bobby couldn't keep his eyes off her.

"Darvi Stanton, this is Staci Galbraith. Staci lives up in Portland. Darvi is new to our community. She just moved here. She's working with Rance on the renovation of the inn."

Darvi held out her hand and offered her best professional smile. "It's a pleasure to meet you, Staci. I must tell you, that's a lovely tan you have. Surely, you didn't acquire that in Portland at this time of year."

Staci shook Darvi's hand as she replied with the unbridled enthusiasm of youth, "In Portland? Not a chance. We just got back from Hawaii. We were there for two weeks. It was the greatest. Have you ever been there? It was my first time."

Darvi hung on Staci's every word. *We* just got back? *So, Rance took her to Hawaii with him.* "Yes, I've been there twice. It's a great place to kick back, relax, and soak up the sun."

"Hey!" Rance's shout grabbed everyone's attention. "This thing is heavy. Someone give me a hand." Bobby ran over to him and grasped one handle of the large ice chest. The two men carried it back to the table and deposited it with a thud.

Frank opened the lid and pulled out two cans of beer, handing one to Rance. The two men immediately opened the tabs on the cans and took long swigs. They set the cans on the table and licked their lips. In unison, they said, "Ahh." Then they both laughed.

Amy, Staci, and Bobby laughed with them, leaving Darvi feeling slightly perplexed. Amy turned to Darvi and managed to explain between giggles. "It's their silly postgame ritual. They go through that exact procedure after each game, win or lose." Amy whispered conspiratorially, "I think it's one of those silly male bonding things."

Frank quickly spoke up. "Hey, love, we don't make fun of all those silly little female things you and your friends do."

"That, my darling husband, is because we don't have any silly little female rituals." Amy gave her husband a quick yet loving kiss on his cheek as he patted her affectionately on her bottom. They were so obviously a devoted couple, comfortable and secure with each other and their marriage. A ripple of longing darted through Darvi as she watched their closeness, a feeling mixed with an uncomfortable combination of envy and despair.

Out of the corner of her eye, Darvi noticed the questioning expression on Rance's face as he stared at her. She glanced away, embarrassed at being caught with her feelings showing even if it had only lasted for a fleeting moment.

"Is it food yet? I'm starved!" The voice belonged to Jim, the third baseman. He and his wife, Carol, walked toward the picnic table. "I could eat my weight in whatever it is we're having."

Darvi glanced at the approaching couple and noticed Jim's stomach hanging over the waist of his jeans.

With a quick look at Carol, Amy patted Jim on the belly. "It appears you already have."

Carol joined in the good-natured kidding. "And that was just breakfast!" As they laughed with Jim, two other couples arrived at the picnic table.

Everyone eagerly dug into the food, filling their plates while Rance distributed beer and soft drinks. Staci snuck her hand into the cooler from behind Rance and withdrew a can of beer. Without even looking in her direction, he took the beer from her and handed her a soft drink.

Staci pouted a moment, then mumbled, "I'm old enough to make up my own mind about what I want to drink."

"Not when you're with me, young lady. When you're old enough to buy it in the store, then you're old enough to drink it." Rance placed the confiscated can of beer back in the cooler and gave Staci a stern look as he closed the lid. She casually shrugged, took her soft drink, and sat down next to Bobby.

The women listened as the men replayed every inning of the game, the more spectacular plays two and three times each. A high-spirited mood prevailed—everyone laughing, eating, and generally enjoying a carefree, sunny afternoon.

Darvi found the open friendliness of the people comfortable. Everyone made her feel welcome, a part of the group. She was having a good time, glad she had accepted Amy's invitation.

Late afternoon brought a cool breeze off the ocean. The unusually sunny, warm day slipped toward evening.

Staci nervously looked at her watch. Finally, she walked over to Rance. "I need to get back to my car and start for Portland. It's getting late. Would you drive me?"

Darvi spotted the quick knowing look that passed between Amy and Frank and the even quicker one between Frank and Rance.

Frank began gathering his things. "We can drive you to your car, Staci. We have some errands to run, and it's right on our way."

Then Frank turned to Rance. "Hey, buddy, you wouldn't mind collecting all this stuff and dropping it by our place, would you?" He paused as he tried to sound casual. "And give Darvi a lift home?"

"No problem. Glad to do it." Rance turned to Staci. "Now, you drive carefully. I'll see you later." He leaned over, gave her a kiss on the cheek, and watched as she trotted off with Bobby to Amy and Frank's car.

When Staci reached the car, she waved, then shouted, "Goodbye, Uncle Rance."

"Goodbye, Staci." He returned Staci's wave, obviously doing his best to avoid Darvi's reaction to this bit of news.

"*Uncle* Rance? She's your niece?" Darvi couldn't hide her astonishment.

"Of course she's my niece, my older sister's daughter." The look on his face grew stern. "Who in the world did you think she was?" He paused a moment then continued. "She's only seventeen. Surely, you didn't think I'd date someone so young. What kind of a man do you think I am? Some sort of cradle robber?"

Darvi felt the hot crimson on her cheeks as Rance leveled a cool blue-eyed gaze directly at her. "Why I…I mean, I didn't…actually, I wasn't…" She did not know whether to be mad or embarrassed.

He did that to me on purpose—baiting me, teasing me, trying to make me jealous. And most upsetting of all? He had succeeded, a realization that did not sit comfortably with her.

Suddenly, another thought struck her. Amy and Frank had been in on this from the beginning right down to the part where they drove Staci back to her car, leaving Darvi alone with Rance and no other transportation. She glared at him. "You seem to have arranged this quite nicely. What's supposed to happen now?"

Rance wore an expression of feigned innocence that said his integrity had been wounded to the core. "I don't know what you mean." He held her gaze a moment longer. "What I suggest should happen next is that we clean up this mess." He turned to the task at hand, gathering food containers and clearing the picnic area. He glanced at Darvi, cocked his head, raised an eyebrow, and gave her a hard look. "You prefer to watch me work rather than helping clean up our picnic area?"

Darvi grabbed some dishes and shoved them into a picnic basket as she muttered under her breath. "I give up. You're totally impossible."

Rance wisely chose not to respond to her comment.

For what seemed like the millionth time, he questioned what he was doing, or more accurately, *why* he was doing it. He had already spent more time and effort in pursuit of Darvi than he had ever invested in any other woman. She had continually rebuffed all his efforts. Rather than doing what he normally did—accepting it and moving on to greener pastures—he had continually attempted new approaches culminating in this totally absurd scheme that even went so far as to incorporate other people in the ruse. What was there about this difficult woman—this *impossible* woman—that had so completely captured his senses and totally mesmerized him?

Amy had been only too happy to help him with his little scheme. She had been trying to fix Rance up for years and immediately agreed to help. Frank, on the other hand, was a different story. Rance had to threaten to quit the softball team to get Frank's cooperation. It wasn't that Frank had anything against Darvi. He just kept saying that Rance was the last of the truly carefree bachelors, and he didn't want to see him forced into domestic servitude. That comment caused Amy to threaten to make Frank's life miserable. She had even hinted at curtailing certain bedroom activities. It had done the trick.

A twinge of guilt poked at Rance for using Staci that way. He never would have thought of it if she hadn't called early that morning to tell him she wanted to drive down and watch their softball game. Reading between the lines, he knew she didn't care about the softball game. She wanted to see Bobby. But as long as she was in town anyway…

Darvi finished packing away the leftover food and the dishes while Rance gathered all the trash in a plastic trash bag and disposed of it. He grabbed the large cooler, and Darvi took the picnic basket.

Before long, the red sports car moved down a side street, passing neat, well-cared-for older homes. Rance pulled into the driveway of Amy and Frank's house. "Sit tight. I'll take their things around to the back and leave them in the kitchen."

Darvi watched as he crossed the lawn and disappeared around the corner of the house, his body movements strong, yet fluid. She found herself retaining an image of his retreating form even after he had disappeared from sight. A nervous shiver shook her as she sat in the car waiting for him to return.

Her mind drifted back three years, to the first time Jerry had walked into her Laguna Beach studio. His dark curly hair and piercing gray eyes had immediately captured her attention. They had started seeing each other casually—lunch now and then, a drink at the end of the work day, an occasional afternoon at a new gallery showing or a movie.

Their relationship had grown closer, until finally they had become lovers. Darvi knew, in retrospect, that she should have recognized the signs. Whenever she tried to discuss their future, he skillfully changed the subject. He put her off with pretty words, flowery phrases, and empty flattery. He gave her answers that really didn't have any substance. She should have suspected something, but she had been enamored by the attention he showered on her and ignored her nagging concerns.

Having an actual lover rather than occasional sex was something new for Darvi. She had never before experienced the type of lovemaking Jerry introduced to their relationship. She had been a virtual novice when their affair began—not a virgin, just inexperienced due to having devoted all her time to establishing her career. He had been an effective teacher, but she now realized that most of their lovemaking had been for his pleasure, not their mutual enjoyment. Then that horrible night...

The gentle caress against her cheek came from the open car window accompanied by a smooth masculine voice that startled Darvi out of her momentary return to the source of her torment and despair.

"Where were you just now? The look on your face placed you a million miles from here, lost in some sort of private hell." Rance stared at her for a moment, looking searchingly into her eyes as if studying her. "I'm a good listener, Darvi."

The arrogance and the adversarial challenge he seemed to wear like a badge had disappeared. In its place, she saw an open sincerity and concern. She wanted to tell someone, to unburden herself, but she didn't dare trust anyone with such a terrible secret. Her fears kicked in, and she shut down her emotions. This time, however, she did not conceal everything behind her defense mechanism of anger.

Chapter Four

Rance gazed into eyes filled with anxiety, almost a plea for understanding. Then Darvi buried her feelings and put on the mask she wore so expertly.

In an almost childlike voice, she answered, "I'm fine." Then she added, so softly as to be almost inaudible, "Thank you. Maybe sometime…"

He tucked a loose tendril of her copper-colored hair behind her ear, cupped her chin with his hand, and raised her face until he could look into her eyes. "What could possibly have happened to hurt you so deeply you would choose to close yourself off from the world—from life?"

His question went unanswered.

Rance withdrew his hand, walked around the car to the driver's side, and slid in behind the wheel. "I'd better get you home. The breeze is turning cooler." He perused her long, bare legs, the shorts she wore, and the outline of her firm breasts beneath her T-shirt. "Besides, you're not exactly dressed for warmth."

A shy smile turned the corners of her mouth. "Neither are you."

When they reached her place, he carried the large bowl that had contained her potato salad and the serving spoon as he walked with her to the door of her studio rather than just dropping her off at the curb. As she inserted the key into the lock, he quickly covered her hand with his. "Here, let me do that."

He had expected her to yank her hand away at his touch. He was pleasantly surprised when her hand lingered before she slowly withdrew it. He unlocked the door and looked inside the room. Once he determined that everything appeared to be okay, he stepped aside, then followed her through the door, closing it behind him. He immediately took the empty bowl and spoon to the kitchen, set them on the counter, and returned to the front door.

Darvi had not intended to let Rance come in, especially after the dirty trick he had pulled on her that afternoon. What she didn't want to acknowledge but couldn't deny was that she had been pleased he had gone to all that trouble just to be able to drive her home, especially after she had been continuously antagonistic toward him. She even forgave Amy and Frank for their part in the deception.

Before she lost her nerve, Darvi whirled around to face him, offering a tentative smile. "Would you like some coffee or tea? It won't take but a moment for me to fix it."

The surprise in his eyes gave way to pleasure. "I'd like that very much. Coffee, if that's okay."

"Coffee it is. Make yourself comfortable. I'll be right back."

Darvi busied herself in the kitchen making coffee, gathering cups, and finding a serving tray to carry all of it. She tried not to dwell on the fact that she had let down her guard, allowed Rance into her personal domain for a nonbusiness purpose, had even been the one to suggest he stay for coffee. She knew if she stopped to consider her actions, she would ask Rance to leave, removing all temptation.

She paused for a moment, her brow furrowed in concentration. Panic stabbed through her as she looked toward the studio where he waited. *Temptation*—exactly what he represented, an overwhelming temptation to which she must not succumb.

She glanced down at her hands, surprised by the way they trembled. Her eyes misted as she fought back the tears. *I can't become involved with him. I could never tell him about what happened. He would never understand about…*

A loud crash filled the air. Darvi stood in the middle of the kitchen, staring blankly at the tray and broken coffee cups at her feet. Tears rolled down her cheeks as the emotional pain and fear surged through her veins. Her entire body trembled.

A moment later, Rance appeared at the kitchen door, a combination of concern, caution, and confusion covering his face. He hesitated for a moment as if not sure what to do, then rushed to her. He pulled her into his arms, placed his hand gently at the back of her head, and cradled it against his shoulder. She couldn't stop the tremors as he held her tightly.

After a long, silent moment, she tentatively reached her arms around his waist and held on, gaining comfort from his strength and closeness. Several seconds passed before she pulled back in an effort to extricate herself from his embrace. The warmth and security of his arms felt good—much too good. Although unsure about how or why she had allowed the intimate situation to happen, she could not allow it to continue.

As she struggled to be free of his embrace, he tightened his hold on her. "No, you don't. This time I'm not letting you run away."

She clenched her fists with a renewed determination and pushed against his hard chest. "How dare you try to hold me here against my will." Her voice quavered as she fought back more tears. "How many times do I need to tell you that nothing's wrong? I'm fine."

His eyes narrowed as his gaze pierced through to her core. "I guess you'll just have to keep telling me until I believe it." His voice projected his total control of the situation. A hint of sarcasm crept into his tone. "And at the rate we're going, that could take years." He moved his hand up her back to the copper-colored French braid, then worked at releasing the clasp holding it together.

Her muscles relaxed as some of the tension drained from her body. He combed his fingers through her long, thick hair as the braid unraveled and the tresses fell around her shoulders. "Come on, let's go to the other room." He edged her toward the kitchen door.

"No, wait…" Her gaze darted around the kitchen, frantically searching for some sort of life line she could grab. "I…" She stared at the broken cups on the floor. "I have to clean up this mess."

"It's not going anywhere. It'll still be here later. Come on." Rance gently, but firmly, escorted her out of the kitchen and to the couch. He turned her face toward him and maintained eye contact for what seemed like forever before he spoke. "Now, start at the beginning. Tell me what happened."

Darvi actually felt protected, cared for, and comforted—a strange feeling, one she had not experienced in a long time. However, giving in to that feeling, permitting him into the turmoil of her life, could only end with more pain, hurt, and emotional upheaval. Tears welled in her eyes as images from the past flashed through her mind. Once again, her body trembled.

How can I tell him? The doctor said it wasn't my fault, I shouldn't blame myself. He was wrong. The psychologist said it wasn't my fault, and I shouldn't blame myself. She was wrong, too. They were both wrong. How can I tell Rance the truth, that I was responsible for the death of my baby!

Tears slipped down her cheeks as she tried to control the rush of panic rapidly welling inside her to the point where it didn't leave room for anything else.

He tentatively nestled her head to his shoulder again as he stroked her hair. "Whatever this is," his voice tender as he talked to her, "it's destructive, and you can't continue to carry it around with you."

"Stop trying to get into my head. There's nothing there that's any of your business." She spoke haltingly, not sure of her words. "You've been pushing me ever since we met. I don't think we should—" She tensed as she tried to escape his hold on her.

"Okay. We don't need to talk right now. We'll just sit here for a little while and get comfortable with each other." He held her tightly, but not so tight that she felt as if she was being restrained or he was forcing her.

A calm settled over Darvi. His touch and soft words soothed her as she nestled in his arms. He was really nice when he wanted to be—gentle, caring, considerate. And incredibly sexy. Her eyelids grew heavy as the upheaval took its toll on her emotions. She drifted toward sleep. Her last conscious thought asked whether she could really trust this man—trust him not to turn against her or be disgusted at her actions and abandon her if she told him the truth. She had a vague impression of Rance shifting his weight slightly as he moved her into a more comfortable position, then darkness prevailed.

Rance watched as she slept peacefully in his arms. Her long red hair framed her beautiful face and fanned out over her shoulders. She was truly lovely. He found himself in the unaccustomed position of offering emotional support. It had been years since he had extended himself this way. Now, the resulting anxiety left him uncertain and unsettled. He allowed a fleeting thought about her anger being a symptom of someone with deep psychological problems, someone in need of professional help.

He dismissed the possibility. No—that wasn't the case. Something happened to her, something devastating. She looked so in need of comfort, a need that touched his own carefully guarded vulnerability. Something they had in common? Even though he had tried to keep that vulnerability buried inside him where no one could touch it, he couldn't fight the pull of her obvious need.

He wondered again why she had left Southern California to settle in the small coastal town of Sandy Cove, Oregon. Other than having the Pacific Ocean in common, the two places couldn't be more different. It almost seemed as if she had been running away from something, but was it real danger or something imagined? Although he could not explain it, did not understand why it should be so, for some reason he felt the need to help her exorcise the demons obviously haunting her.

Like it or not, he had just taken his first step into uncharted territory. He didn't know where his personal involvement with this tantalizing woman would take him. A small tremor of anxiety assaulted his senses. One thing for sure—he was stepping outside his comfort zone. His conscious decision seemed to be in direct conflict with what his deeply held determinations tried to tell him. He continued to hold her while she slept. His aching muscles screamed at him, saying he had maintained his awkward position too long. In spite of the discomfort, he dared not move for fear of disturbing her.

Her breathing suddenly became labored, her peaceful features contorted in anguish. He jerked to attention. A strange combination of anxiety and concern forced its way back into his consciousness. She thrashed about, turning her head from side to side as if trying to ward off some terrible evil. "Darvi…are you okay? Talk to me!"

She mumbled something, but he couldn't make it out. A moment of panic grabbed him as her agitation increased. He tried to think logically. She was obviously having a bad dream, a nightmare of some sort. He had no idea what to do. Should he wake her?

He went with instinct, pulling her body tightly against his and rocking her in his arms. He stroked her hair. "Darvi, it's okay. Don't worry."

Darvi's face softened. Her breathing gradually returned to normal. An audible sigh of relief escaped his throat. Whatever had invaded her sleep and caused her such terror seemed to have gone. He studied the way she nestled in his arms.

A warm feeling spread through him as he tentatively allowed his own deeply buried feelings to surface. Someone *needed* him. *She* needed him. It had been more years than he could remember since anyone truly needed him. He readily admitted part of that came from purposely keeping his interactions with women he dated on a strictly casual level. On the other hand, the needy clinging vine type of woman genuinely represented a major turn off for him, a dynamic very different from someone genuinely needing him on a much deeper level.

He frowned as he did mental battle with himself over what to do, not at all sure he was doing the right thing. Was this foray into unknown territory taking on more than he wanted to handle or, specifically, more than he was able to handle?

The sun dropped from sight and darkness pervaded through her studio. The only illumination came from the bright moonlight filtering through the window. She stirred, and he immediately tightened his hold on her.

Darvi shook the grogginess from her head as she opened her eyes and tried to focus in the darkness. Confusion swirled through her mind. Where was she? What happened? Then everything came rushing back to her.

"What time is it?" Her wariness crept into her voice. "How long have I been sleeping? Why is it so dark in here?"

"In order—it's almost nine o'clock, about three hours, and I didn't want to disturb you by getting up to turn on a light." He brushed a stray tendril from her cheek. "I like your hair down like this. It adds an extra softness."

Panic—her first reaction told her to put some distance between herself and this very tempting man. But for some inexplicable reason, she did not move from the couch. She felt warm and safe in his arms, a sensation she had not experienced in a long time. "I don't wear my hair down because it gets in my way when I work." Her words were tentative, not at all sure if she should say them. "Once, I sealed the ends into a window when I was soldering a piece of glass in place. I finally had to cut off the ends of my hair to get free. Fortunately, what I was working on was something for me rather than for a client."

A tremor of anxiety flitted across her skin, followed by a moment of nervousness. She looked around the darkened room searching for anything she could grasp to return the situation to neutral ground. "I think we should turn on some lights."

He eased her away from him, then stood up and stretched his arms above his head. He snapped on a table lamp. "It's getting chilly in here. Where's the thermostat?"

"In the hall." Darvi shivered as the cool air hit her bare arms and legs in sharp contrast to the warmth of Rance's arms. "Excuse me for a minute, I'll be right back."

She hurried to her bedroom, this time making sure the door was completely closed. Her mind reeled as she sank onto the bed.

What have I gotten myself into? Her uncertainty and turmoil played havoc with her logic. She sat a moment longer then changed into an old sweatshirt and sweatpants. She finished by pulling on a pair of warm socks.

Her mind darted from one thing to another in an attempt to sort out conflicting thoughts. They had been at odds over many things, but she had to reluctantly admit that Rance had been correct about one thing. She couldn't continue to run away from her demons.

She had run from Southern California to Oregon, but her demons had followed. She couldn't run away for the rest of her life. Or more accurately, she couldn't run away from life. She needed to face up to her fears and somehow manage to conquer them. Just because her relationship with Jerry ended in an agonizingly painful and emotionally devastating manner didn't mean that another relationship would follow the same path.

She released a slight bittersweet laugh. Besides, she was older now. And hopefully *much* wiser.

She thought back to Rance's kiss on the patio of the art gallery. He had called it right—she wanted him to kiss her. But as soon as the kiss had turned from physical to emotional, she became frightened. At that instant, she had realized the magnitude of her attraction to him…and how much the possible consequences terrified her.

Darvi took a deep, steadying breath. What would happen if she stopped trying to keep him at arm's length? Nothing could be as painful as what she had already been through. It could not hurt as much as Jerry's total betrayal of her trust and what she had thought at that time was love. Nothing could hurt her as much as the loss of her baby.

She opened the bedroom door and returned to the kitchen. Rance had cleaned up the broken coffee cups during her absence and now stood in front of the open refrigerator door staring at the contents. He reached for an opened bottle of white wine and poured himself a glass.

"You could pour me one of those, too, if you don't mind." Her eyes drifted over his body—hard chest, broad shoulders, muscular arms and legs. He was, indeed, a sexy and physically desirable man. It had been a long time since she had allowed herself to acknowledge the purely physical desire. She could no longer bury those needs.

Maybe he'll be able to… I hope he can understand about…

She shook her head. She wanted to tell him about Jerry, about the baby—about everything. But she wouldn't tell him for a while, not until she felt more comfortable with him and the situation, more confident that he was not really the arrogant jerk he seemed determined to present to the world at large. Trust was a difficult thing for her. It no longer came easily, if at all. She needed to have someone she could trust, someone she could confide in. She wanted to trust him. But did she dare? She made the uneasy decision to try.

Rance stared at Darvi, taking in every nuance. She had run a brush through her hair. The long tresses flowed around her shoulders. Something about her—perhaps the look in her eyes—appeared somehow different. She seemed calmer, more relaxed. He sensed a new vulnerability, an openness that hadn't been there until now. A sudden jolt of panic hit him, as if she had physically reached out and grabbed hold of his reality and refused to let go. He had been pushing her to talk to him. Now, he wasn't so sure about it.

He picked up another wineglass, uncertainty running rampant about how to treat the situation. His manner stiffened as he pointed to the floor.

"I cleaned up your mess for you." A sharp edge clung to his voice, something he hadn't intended…almost like an involuntary self-defense mechanism. He poured a glass of wine and sucked in a steadying breath as he handed it to her.

Darvi took the glass from his hand. She glanced at the floor. "I'm sorry about the mess." She looked up, catching his gaze before quickly looking away again. "Thank you for—"

"Come on." He cut her off in mid sentence as an uncomfortable tightness pulled across his chest. "Let's sit down and talk."

Grabbing her hand, he led her back to the couch and sat next to her. He was about to launch himself into the realm of sharing, understanding, and patience with a woman he found very attractive and desirable, a place he had worked hard to avoid for the last ten years. She was also a troubled woman but not in the sense of someone with dangerous psychological problems.

He had reached one definite conclusion, her fears and avoidance of anything that touched her buried vulnerability seemed to parallel his own inner turmoil. He used a façade of aggression and control with a touch of arrogance to hide behind while she had chosen to hide behind a wall of anger. He tried to force a calm to the anxiety churning in his stomach. He related to her apprehension, perhaps too closely. She nervously toyed with her glass. Her obvious distress elicited a surprisingly emotional reaction from him, one that frightened him, one he instantly tried to quell.

One he identified with and knew well.

She finally spoke. "You said you wanted to talk. What do you want to talk about?"

"I want to talk about you." He instantly became aware of the cool, almost analytical, tone in his voice, not at all the quality to induce a feeling of confidence in someone. He struggled with his own conflicts as he watched her growing anxiety.

She took a deep breath, held it for a second, then slowly exhaled. She finally started to speak, her words cloaked in defensiveness. "I had my life under control until I ran into you. I'm taking care of some simple errands and you turn it into a major confrontation over some stupid parking spot on a public street. You've been going out of your way to antagonize me at every opportunity. I know you wanted George to hire someone else to do the stained glass, but he hired me in spite of your objections. I have a signed contract. The least you can do is make an effort to be decent about it."

Her words caught him off guard. "I don't have any—"

"I'm not a helpless little thing who cries at the drop of a hat. I've always been able to take care of myself, handle any situation that came along. You're pushing me too hard, asking too much...*demanding* too much, things that have nothing to do with you or with this job. Things that are none of your business."

The tears welled in her eyes as her veneer began to crumble. "You apparently believe that I should just trust you because you say so even though you've done nothing to show me your sincerity or that you can actually be trusted. How do I know what your intentions are? Why should I believe that you will keep anything I say to you in confidence rather than using it to humiliate me? Stop pushing me so hard. It's very difficult for me...very painful."

The arrogant Rance persona started to speak, the spontaneous outburst coming out as a harsh sound. "Pushing you? I haven't—" The rest of the sentence stuck in his throat. His totally inappropriate reaction to what she said meshed with his own unspoken fears. He pulled her into his embrace as a mass of apprehension swirled around inside him. What to think...what to do…he didn't have any answers. He stroked her hair as he thought over what she had said. He had no idea he had been pushing her that hard. Or that she harbored a secret so frightening for her that even what he thought of as teasing banter had been too painful for her to handle.

And her comment about not trusting him, fearing he would turn her secret against her in such a callous manner… He didn't like hearing it, knew he would never do such a thing, but quickly realized why she would think it.

It was a real eye-opener for him, obviously a major concession on her part to have revealed as much as she did. Her words sank in, making one thing more than obvious. He had been behaving like a total ass. Her accusation of arrogance didn't even begin to accurately describe it. He needed to back off and give her room. She would tell him what she could when she was ready. And apparently, that wouldn't be until she could trust his discretion. A heavy dose of guilt, regret, and shame surged through him. He may have come off as a jerk, but he would never betray someone's deeply held confidence.

"You're right. I have been less than gracious. I owe you an apology."

Darvi stared at him as she turned his comment over in her mind, waiting for him to continue, but he didn't say anything else. "You say you owe me an apology, but apparently, you don't intend to actually apologize."

A big smile quickly spread across his face. "I apologize, Darvi. I'm sorry for behaving like…as you put it…an arrogant jerk. However, I think jackass might have been a more appropriate word." His smile faded to be replaced by a sincere moment. "Forgive me?"

The spontaneous laugh escaped her throat before she could quell the urge. "Who could resist or argue with that sad little puppy dog expression? Yes, I'll forgive you..." her expression turned serious, "as long as you promise not to do it again."

He stuck out his hand toward her. "Friends?"

She hesitated, then accepted his handshake. "Yes, friends."

"So, you know I'm from Portland. How about you? Are you originally from California? From Laguna Beach specifically? Or like so many Californians, are you a transplant from somewhere else?"

"I've lived in Southern California for my entire life. I was born in Santa Monica and eventually moved to Laguna Beach. I moved here recently. This is a charming little town, and I definitely do not miss the California traffic, congestion, and the super expensive cost of living."

"Laguna is certainly an artist's area. How did you get involved with stained glass?"

She allowed a shy smile to tug at the corners of her mouth as she recalled the memory. "I was fifteen years old and went to an exhibit of stained glass and watched an artist go through the motions of making a wall hanging. I fell in love with it and decided that was what I wanted to do. The biggest hurdle to overcome was trying to get established and making it a career rather than a hobby."

"What about your family? Any brothers or sisters?"

"No, I'm an only child."

"As you know...you met Staci this afternoon...I have an older sister who lives in Portland with her husband and three kids. Staci is their oldest."

****

The pendulum clock chimed midnight. In spite of an occasional clash of wills during the course of the evening, they had spent almost three hours talking and laughing. Darvi was a different person than Rance had previously experienced, open as long as the conversation didn't become too personal. Witty, charming, intelligent…a joy to be with. He asked himself several times why this delightful woman had chosen to hide behind that wall of anger.

He glanced at the clock as it sounded the hour. "I can't believe it's this late." He eyed her longingly for a brief moment, then returned his attention to reality. "I'd better leave and let you get some sleep." They walked to the front door together. "Besides, if I don't get my car out from in front of your place, the local gossips will have us as an item before breakfast is over."

His gaze lingered on her mouth as he leaned against the front door. He took her face in his hands and held it before lowering his head. His mouth brushed hers, then he captured her parted lips. He drank in her tantalizing sweetness, a taste uniquely hers. He reveled in the softness of her lips, the texture of her mouth, the excitement of their tongues touching.

Her breathing quickened to match his. The firmness of her full breasts pressed against his chest as her hands gently stroked the length of his back. He marveled at her sensuality. His passions surged toward an uncontrollable vortex. They needed to stop while he still had control of his physical desires.

Easier said than done.

Darvi melted into Rance's arms as he embraced her. She allowed his mouth to envelope her in the exquisite kiss, his lips nibbling, teasing, devouring. His tongue probed the darkness of her mouth, searching, and exploring. He made her feel things she thought she would never feel again, longings she thought she had managed to bury never to be resurrected.

The pull of his passion told her making love with him would be unlike anything she had ever experienced or even imagined in her wildest flights of fantasy. But they had to stop before it was too late, before she gave in to the desire rapidly building between them.

She pulled back from his embrace and saw the smoky blue passion in the depth of his eyes as he caressed her cheek with his fingertips. She had trouble finding her voice. Finally, she spoke, her breathless words difficult to formulate. "I...I think you should—" He brushed his lips against hers again, sending tingling sensations through her body. "—uh, leave before it gets any later."

He again captured her mouth with a force that left her weak in the knees and almost limp in his arms. She trembled as she pressed her body against his.

"Yes, I think you're right." He released her, but his body language said he didn't want to. He held her face in his hands, his touch conveying both emotion and tenderness as he looked searchingly into her eyes. "You're very special, Darvi Stanton. Don't let anyone try to tell you differently, including me. Don't ever sell yourself short."

"Thank you." She wanted to thank him for his apparent decision to understand. The last few hours had been delightful. But was that a reality or only her desire for it to be true?

His muscles tensed. A stern look crossed his face as

his entire persona changed right before her eyes. "We're not through talking about this." His voice had lost the soft edge that had just been there. "Don't think you can get away with working your charms on me like that and think I'll just drop it."

His words shocked her, especially coming immediately after the passionate kiss they had shared. "Me? I'm not the one who initiated the kiss—"

"I'd better get out of here." He opened the door, ran quickly through the cold night air, climbed in his car, and drove down the dark street.

She leaned against the closed front door, shut her eyes, and put her fingertips to her lips. Confusion swirled inside her. What just happened? Everything had been going so well. Then all of a sudden he'd transformed from the tender, caring, sensual man who had been with her for the last few hours into the arrogant, insensitive jerk who had rudely confronted her about a parking space. Which of those two identities depicted the real Rance Coulter?

She walked to her bedroom, quickly undressed, climbed into bed, and pulled the down comforter up to her chin then closed her eyes. Perhaps it would be best to stay as far away as possible from a man with such abrupt mood swings. At the moment, trusting him seemed like a very bad idea.

She tried to separate her emotional fears from logic and reality. Could her fears and attempts to cover them be considered mood swings of sorts to someone not familiar with her past? Could Rance have something equally troubling in his past that would explain his behavior? Or could she, once again, be over analyzing something in an attempt to find ready answers to her turmoil? Answers that weren't available?

She finally fell asleep, but it was not peaceful.

****

Rance pulled his car into the garage. He sat behind the wheel for a long time, his brow furrowed as he berated himself for the manner in which he had left Darvi's studio. She had not deserved that type of brusque behavior. He didn't even know exactly what prompted him to behave that way. Something about her touched him on a deeply emotional level, and that something scared the hell out of him. He lived by the rule of never letting his guard down with women, always keeping things casual, always staying a step ahead of the game. But with Darvi, he found himself violating that rule even if only momentarily.

He tried to put some rational thought to what happened. What had he opened himself up to by trying to dig into her past, by insisting she confide in him? He didn't have a clue what to do. Should he push or back off? Let her have her own time frame? And for that matter, exactly what gave him the right to pry into her personal life? How would he respond if the situation was reversed? If she insisted on digging into his private agony?

It was a question he preferred not to explore, one better left alone.

Chapter Five

Darvi lay in bed as the morning sun streamed in around the edge of her bedroom drapes. She stretched out her long legs, wiggled her toes, and rolled over onto her stomach. It had all the makings of another unseasonably warm day.

Thoughts of Rance Coulter invaded her mind. Last night, in spite of his abrupt departure, she had made the surprising decision to trust him. In the bright light of day, without the distraction of his closeness, perhaps she needed to rethink that notion.

Arrogant, pushy, demanding, even occasionally rude—not qualities she looked for in a friend and certainly not qualities that instilled trust.

And definitely not ones that could lead to a relationship.

She shook away the strange thought as an involuntary frown wrinkled across her forehead. *Relationship?* Where had that word come from?

But then he turned around and had been tender, caring, and understanding. She raised her fingertips to her lips remembering the sensation of his kiss. A smile curled the corners of her mouth. Her decision would stand. She would trust him in spite of all the reasons why she shouldn't.

Now that she had settled the matter in her mind, she vowed to stick with that decision. A lightness of spirit she had not experienced in a long time settled over her. She threw back the covers and climbed out of bed. Energy flowed through her. The prospect of a new day excited her. She looked forward to whatever it had in store.

****

Rance opened his eyes and focused on the clock by his bed. Eleven o'clock. It had been a little before five that morning when he left his workshop and finally went to bed. Six hours sleep would do. He had often functioned on less. But as for today, the day was almost half gone. He headed for the shower.

He emerged from his bathroom dripping water across the floor. The hot shower had taken some of the kinks out of his muscles. The first softball game of the season always made him sore. He refused to entertain the possibility it might be because he had moved beyond his twenties and into his mid thirties. He did not exercise as much as he should. He hardly ever went jogging any more. His job provided physical activity but didn't use the same muscles as he used when playing softball.

He dressed quickly, then reached for the phone. He waited impatiently as the phone rang, not knowing what type of reception he would receive, especially after last night's abrupt departure. Three, four, five rings. Darvi finally answered. "Hello?"

"Have you had breakfast yet?"

"Breakfast? It's almost noon. Did you just get up?"

"Don't be ridiculous. Of course not. Obviously, I meant to say brunch. Have you had brunch yet?"

"I haven't eaten if that's what you're trying to ask." Her laugh was warm and open. "Whatever meal you want to call it."

"Good! I'll pick you up in fifteen minutes." Before she could say yes or no, he terminated the phone connection.

****

It seemed that everybody in town had decided to take advantage of the unseasonably warm, sunny weather. The outside dining patio at the Wine Bistro didn't have an empty table. Rance and Darvi made their way through the crowd to a table for six next to the railing looking over the ocean. Amy, Frank, Jim, and Carol were already seated and enjoying their Sunday brunch champagne.

Frank called out to Rance as he held up his almost empty champagne glass. "As you can see, we waited for you." He glanced at Darvi, his expression one of genuine guilt about participating in Rance's scheme following the softball game.

Darvi's warm, outgoing smile assured Frank she didn't harbor any hard feelings.

Everyone exchanged greetings as Jim filled the two remaining champagne glasses. Rance turned toward Darvi, clinked his glass to hers, and took a sip of champagne. His eyes never left her face. The heat of embarrassment spread across her cheeks as she lowered her eyelids and raised the glass to her lips.

Brunch moved along happily, everyone laughing and talking. Jim made two trips to the buffet. When he rose to make his third, Carol stopped him.

"Jim, enough is enough."

"But honey, it says *all you can eat*. I'm still hungry."

Carol gave an exasperated sigh. "I'll fix you something when we get home." Jim sat down in his chair, a disappointed look on his face.

During the course of the meal Rance had casually inched his chair closer and closer to Darvi's. His right hand and her left hand were both hidden under the table, their fingers laced together in a warm and intimate manner.

Finally, Jim and Carol moved to break up their group. Carol looked at Jim as she slowly shook her head. "I've got to get him home and feed him. He's only had two meals so far today and here it is…already two o'clock."

Jim grinned self-consciously. "I have to keep up my strength." He shot a quick, lustful look in Carol's direction, then turned his attention to the rest of the group. "Who knows, I might even get lucky this afternoon."

Carol rolled her eyes in mock irritation, but an impish grin slowly crossed her face. "We'd better get out of here while he's still in the mood."

Everyone laughed as Carol and Jim said their goodbyes and made their way across the patio.

Amy quickly gathered her purse and stood up. "I hate to abandon you two, but Frank and I have several things to do today. We'd better get started."

Frank gave his wife a confused look. "What things?"

Amy shot him a look that only a husband could understand.

"Oh, yeah. Those things." Frank quickly rose to his feet and the couple departed after a few minutes of idle chitchat.

Darvi and Rance remained at the table. She sipped the last of her coffee.

He watched her closely. "Would you like some more?"

She pushed the cup and saucer across the table. "No way. I don't know where I'd put it." She looked up at him. His gaze captured her in its spell. Once again, he seemed to be exerting some sort of mystical power over her. And once again, the arrogance had disappeared. In its place, she felt the warmth and caring that made her pulse race with excitement.

"If you're sure you don't want anything else, I guess we'd better leave." He rose from his seat and held her chair for her as she stepped away from the table.

Rance placed his hand against her back, eliciting a quick ripple of desire as her immediate response to the physical contact. He guided her across the patio, through the restaurant, and out to the parking lot. When they reached his sports car, he wrapped both arms around her and leaned her back against the car door. Her pulse quickened as he looked intently into her eyes. Then he lowered his mouth to hers.

Darvi hesitated as their lips brushed. She quickly regained her composure and pulled her head away from his. "What do you think you're doing, right here in the parking lot of a busy restaurant?" Surprise filled her voice. "I thought you were worried about the local tongues wagging with gossip."

He lightly drew his fingertips across the smooth skin of her cheek as he continued to encircle her with his other arm. "I think we're too late. Didn't you notice, my pet, how quickly everyone deserted us after we finished eating?"

My pet? Darvi stiffened at the sound of the words. Jerry had called her by that particular *endearment*. The expression truly rankled her.

Rance straightened. "What's wrong?"

"Nothing." She spat out a reply as she attempted to move away from him.

His firm determination overruled her anger. He quickly grabbed her shoulders and used his body to trap her against the car, preventing her from turning and leaving. "Don't think you can tell me nothing's wrong and get away with it." He searched her face for some answers. "Everything was fine, then suddenly you're shooting daggers at me. What did I say to upset you? What did I do?" He paused to collect his thoughts. "Talk to me, Darvi. I can't be constantly worried that I'm going to innocently say something that will set off your anger unless I know what the potential danger areas are."

Darvi glared at him for a minute, then spoke, her voice a mixture of anger and hurt. "I'm not your *pet*, nor am I your plaything or your property."

Guilt stabbed at him as he realized exactly what he had said, and more to the point, how she had interpreted it. It certainly had not been his intention to imply any such thing. He studied her defiant glare. Slowly, he wrapped his arms around her again, drawing her to him. At first, she offered some resistance, then she folded into his embrace.

"No, you're not any of those things." He kissed her tenderly on the cheek. "I unintentionally made a bad choice of words. I'm sorry." He seldom apologized for minor things and certainly not for an innocent comment said without malice or malicious intent.

"I'm sorry, too." Her voice softened to a near whisper. "I've made a big deal about nothing—once again."

He looked intently into her eyes, still searching for answers. "It obviously wasn't *nothing* from your perspective. Is that part of what this is about? Someone from your past—some man—treated you that way?" He embraced her tightly, stroking her hair as he cradled her head against his shoulder. He sensed her need for care and understanding, not badgering. "It's going to be okay. We'll work this out."

She trembled slightly as he leaned against her. Finally, Darvi raised her head and gazed into his honest blue eyes. She offered him a shy smile. "I'm okay. Really, I am."

He leaned down and kissed her tenderly on the lips, then looked into her troubled face, not at all sure how far to push her, especially after her outburst the previous evening about him constantly badgering her. "Who was he? Who was the bastard who did this to you?"

She hesitated, then the words came out quietly, almost inaudibly. "His name is Jerry Peterson. I met him one warm sunny afternoon three years ago when he wandered into my studio in Laguna Beach. He was twenty years older than me—charming, captivating, dynamic…and forceful."

Rance jerked to attention. *Forceful? Did this low life slime force her? Had he raped her?*

His arms involuntarily tightened around her. His heart pounded wildly. He tried to keep his voice calm. He did not want Darvi to jump to the wrong conclusion by thinking he was angry with her or blaming her.

"This Jerry Peterson, did he…uh…force you—" He didn't know what to say, how to verbalize his thoughts.

She placed her fingers on his lips. "No, that's not what happened, not what I meant, not what you're thinking." Her voice contained a sense of urgency, a need to get across her point. "There wasn't any physical coercion." She rested her head against his shoulder and did not say another word. Several minutes passed in silence as he cradled her in his arms.

Rance didn't know what to do, whether to simply hold her, encourage her to continue talking, or put her in the car and drive her home.

She made the decision for him. She slowly extricated herself from his embrace and peered around the parking lot. She looked into his eyes, gave him a tentative smile, and lightly touched his cheek. "We should leave before we start drawing a crowd."

He reached up and captured her hand in his. It bothered him that there had been something so traumatic in her past that it could have such an adverse impact on her life. That it could be an obstacle between them. He had given it a lot of thought. He wanted to know more about her because he genuinely cared about her. Where all of this might lead still scared him, but he had warmed to the possibility of some sort of a relationship, one not based on sex and nothing else.

"We're going to talk. Where would you like to go, your place or mine?" He saw the uncertainty enter her eyes. She started to say something, but he stopped her. "Before you offer me a multitude of excuses, let me tell you something."

He looked at her, plumbed the depths of her consciousness as he collected his words. "We're going somewhere right now, and we're going to talk this out. Nothing is as bad when you share it in the light of day as it is when you keep it hidden in a dark closet, afraid to let it out. That fear feeds on darkness. It grows and grows until it becomes overwhelming and ends up taking over your life."

She glanced down at the ground and back to his face. A sigh of resignation escaped her lips. "You're not going to let this go, are you? You're going to hound me until you have what you want." Her eyes searched, both questioning and frightened. "And after you have what you want—then what? What happens, Rance, if I tell you everything you want to know, and you find it as horrible as I know it is? What if you aren't able to accept and forgive what happened? Then what, Rance? Then what?"

Surprise darted through him. This was not what he had expected her to say. He studied her for a long moment. "What could possibly be that terrible?"

"You're asking me to relive the most horrible thing that ever happened to me, that will ever happen to me. You're asking me to bring it out in the open, to relive all the pain and hurt, to once again experience the horror. And you're expecting me to do this on blind faith, just because you say *trust me*."

Darvi's voice took on a hard, bitter edge. Her eyes narrowed as they grew distant and angry. "I've heard *trust me* before. I've heard it said with all the sincerity and caring possible to inject into those two words. And I was so naïve back then that I believed it."

"You don't want to bring it out into the open? Don't want to be forced to relive the emotional turmoil?" He shook his head. "Don't you see that you're already doing it to yourself. You torture yourself with it. You literally live it over and over every day."

Darvi felt herself being drawn into the honesty in Rance's eyes. Everything he said to her made sense—logically. But emotionally? None of it made sense. She felt as if her life was being torn apart.

Tears welled in her eyes. Confusion and uncertainty

churned inside her. She squeezed her eyelids tightly shut as the anguish nearly overwhelmed her. She tried to speak, but words would not come out.

She tried again, forcing the words, her voice small and frightened. "I want to trust you, Rance. Really, I do. But…it's just that…" She opened her eyes and held his gaze for an instant then lowered it. "Can we please go? Will you take me home?"

"Of course, I'll drive you home." They got in his car, and he drove out of the parking lot headed for her house.

Rance parked in front. He took her key from her and unlocked the door, stepping aside so she could enter the studio.

She immediately turned to face him, blocking his way. "Thank you for brunch."

"No, you don't." He grabbed her around the waist, literally lifted her off the floor, and set her to one side. She stood in stunned silence as he came in, closed the door, and turned to face her. He took her hands in his and led her to the couch. After seating her in the corner, he sat down next to her. He didn't say anything, watching her as she wrestled with her shifting emotions and the dilemma he had forced on her.

Darvi nervously clasped and unclasped her hands, twirled an errant strand of hair, and took a steadying breath. Her gaze darted around the room before it returned to Rance. He put his arm around her shoulders, sharing his strength as he gave her both physical and emotional support.

She closed her eyes, afraid to look at him. Her heart pounded with anxiety. The words came out slowly, tentatively. "Like I said, he was dynamic, forceful. I'd never met anyone like him. My experience with men was limited. I had spent most of my time and energy trying to get my career on track. I wasn't part of the beach partying crowd or the singles bar scene. I didn't date much. He just sort of swept me off my feet. It was easy for him—flowers, lots of compliments, pretty words. He buried me in attention and flattery. No one had ever treated me like that before, paid that kind of attention to me, made me feel so special."

She took another steadying breath. "Can you comprehend how that could happen?" Her eyes silently pleaded for understanding. "At first, we saw each other casually, once or twice a week. We would have lunch, sometimes attend a gallery showing, occasionally go to a movie matinee. This went on for a couple of months. He would call me almost every day, whether we saw each other or not. He began to make his intentions clear, the direction he wanted our relationship to take. He planned our future." A sob caught in her throat. "At least, that's what I thought he was doing, planning a future for us filled with only good things."

Tears slipped silently down her cheeks. He kissed her forehead and held her closer. She took a deep breath in an attempt to steady her nerves before continuing.

"He became jealous of my time and my friends. With the exception of my work, he soon had me isolated from almost everything and everyone who had been part of my life before we met. I didn't realize what was going on, it all happened so smoothly, so subtly. Some of my friends tried to warn me about him, but I wouldn't listen. I rationalized everything by telling myself anyone who was that attentive and giving couldn't be bad for me. He was someone who had my best interest at heart. It was my friends who were jealous of what I thought was my ideal relationship."

She turned toward Rance. "Only he wasn't a giving, loving man. He was selfish and cruel. Not cruel as in physically abusive. He was psychologically cruel. He tried to make me feel guilty whenever I didn't comply with something he wanted. He would give me a hurt look and say things like, 'I thought you loved me.' To this day, I don't fully understand how I allowed it to happen, how I let him manipulate me like that. Why I didn't see what he was doing?"

Her voice became loud and forceful, filled with the anger she had been carrying inside her. "I don't know why I didn't tell him to go to hell rather than feeling guilty."

She paused to reconsider what she had just said. Then her voice turned soft again. "I guess I thought I was in love with him and that he was in love with me. It was my obligation, my *duty*, to please him…to make him happy. The more things I did, the more he demanded. We had been lovers for almost a year when my world fell apart."

She reached for Rance's hand, grasping it tightly as she sought out his strength. "I simply couldn't believe I was pregnant. The first time we'd made love Jerry told me not to worry about it. I assumed he meant he had a vasectomy. I wasn't secure enough, self-confident enough to demand he explain exactly what *don't worry about it* meant. I should have taken immediate steps to protect myself from becoming pregnant, but I foolishly didn't. Instead, I trusted what he said. It was a miracle that a year passed before I became pregnant. I went to the doctor. I didn't tell Jerry about the appointment. The tests confirmed I was pregnant. It was a week after that before I saw Jerry. He had been out of town on business. At least, that's what he told me."

She shifted her weight a little bit. Her fingernails dug into his skin. "We were at my studio the evening he returned. It had been raining for three days, one of those Southern California winter storms. He saw how nervous I was. He apparently thought the storm was bothering me. I didn't know the proper etiquette for telling a lover I was pregnant, that he was going to be a father."

A hard tremor shuddered through her body. The most painful part of her story remained. She forced out the words before her fears could quiet them.

"In my mind, I saw him throwing his arms around me, telling me how much he loved me, how thrilled he was about the baby. He'd ask me to marry him, and we'd live happily ever after." Her voice became almost a whisper. "I soon found out that was a fairy tale meant only for little girls—little girls and gullible, naïve women."

Rance's heart ached as he listened to her story, the pain in her eyes almost more than be could handle. It had never occurred to him that her turmoil would be so deep-seated, so intensely personal. He continued to hold her, his embrace mechanical more than purposeful. His insides became numb. Her story touched more than his caring and compassion. It exacerbated his own emotional pain and conflicts. He knew the story so well, but he knew it from the other side.

Joan had used that particular ploy to get him to marry her. She had claimed to be pregnant. Even though he did not love her and thought he had taken all necessary precautions, he had done the honorable thing and married her. It didn't take long for him to discover she had lied about the pregnancy. When he confronted her, she had given him a coy smile, batted her long eyelashes, and told him she hoped he wasn't too angry about her *little deception.*

He had done his best to make the marriage work. All his efforts were wasted, however, when seven months later, Joan ran off with a former boyfriend. Rance vowed he would never again allow himself to get so close to a women or become emotionally involved. He had since restricted himself to the fun and games. If it looked like the woman was getting too serious, he broke it off. During the last ten years, he had not once allowed himself to be drawn into an emotional commitment.

Yet here he sat, actually encouraging an emotional situation with a woman who made him feel things he did not want to feel. His inner defense mechanism told him to escape while he could still get out. His basic, decent instincts, however, told him he had pushed her into this confession with unrelenting determination. Now, it was his obligation to stick with her through the ensuing upheaval it had caused—the ensuing upheaval *he* had caused—regardless of how uncomfortable it made him. He forced his attention away from his uncomfortable thoughts and returned it to Darvi. His discomfort was minor compared to her turmoil.

The tears flowed freely from her eyes and streamed down her cheeks. She spoke through her sobs, each word becoming more difficult to say. "I told him straight out I was pregnant. He just stared at me, then let out a cruel chuckle, the expression on his face cold, hard, and totally uncaring. Then he looked away. He said, 'What do you expect me to do about it? You should have been more careful.' I'll never forget those horrible words. They seared themselves into my consciousness and became permanently imprinted on my brain."

She didn't say any more as the sobs consumed her body. He cradled her head against his shoulder and gently rocked her in his arms. With his jaw clenched in anger, he replayed her words in his mind. He was not exactly sure about the source of his anger, whether it stemmed from his own bitter memories of a woman falsely claiming to be pregnant with his child or because this despicable man had turned Darvi's life into a living hell. More likely a combination of both.

She finally pulled away from him and sat up straight. Rance kissed her on the cheek, tasting the saltiness of her tears. He ached as her pain continued to touch him.

Darvi may have been the one reliving the emotional upheaval, but it was Rance who didn't know how much more he could handle. Again, he questioned why he had insisted on pursuing that very dangerous situation with Darvi. An answer tried to present itself, but he refused to allow it. He wasn't sure he really wanted to know.

"You don't need to say anything more right now if you don't want to," he said, his voice warm and caring. "We can talk later, if you'd rather."

Darvi had been using every ounce of strength she could muster to hold back the storm threatening to burst forth from her inner turmoil. She had to tell him the rest while she could still manage the words. She mustered a brave smile. "No, you forced this much out of me. I want to finish it. There's not much more to tell."

She wiped away the tears with her hands as she drew in a steadying breath. "I couldn't believe he'd actually said that. I guess I must have just stood there staring at him, my mouth hanging open. Finally, he stood up and said, 'Surely, you can't be expecting me to marry you.' I was in such a state of shock that my mind went blank. All I could think of was getting as far away from him as quickly as possible. I didn't want to see him, hear his voice, or even be in the same room with him. I turned and ran blindly out the door and into the street. It was dark, raining hard. I ran right into the path of an oncoming car."

Her voice quavered as she continued. "The next thing I remember was waking up in the hospital. I'd been unconscious for two days. The doctor told me I was a very lucky woman. I had sustained a bad concussion, one broken rib and two more that were cracked, and fifteen stitches across my hip. The nurse handed me an envelope and said a man left it for me the night the ambulance brought me to the hospital."

A cold shudder ran through her body. "It was a note from Jerry telling me to get an abortion and a check for five hundred dollars." She fought the sick churning in the pit of her stomach. "The next thing I discovered—the ultimate betrayal—he was married. He had been married all along, and I never knew it."

She turned tear-filled eyes up at Rance. "There was one last final blow. The accident had resulted in a miscarriage. I'd lost my baby."

She couldn't hold back the torrent of tears as they flooded down her cheeks. Her body trembled violently with convulsive sobs. The tears stung her eyes. She squeezed them shut, trying to stop the burning. "Running out into that storm, blindly running into the street without looking, I was responsible for the death of my baby. It was all my fault."

"No! No way were you responsible." He cupped her face in his hands, his thumbs smoothing the tears from her cheeks as he peered into her eyes. "Listen to me." His tone of voice demanded she give him her full attention. "It was not your fault. The miscarriage was an accident. The blame for everything else falls squarely and totally on that bastard who did this to you."

"I...I..." She squeezed her eyes shut again as once more her body convulsed with violent tremors.

He wrapped his arms tightly around her and stroked her long hair. "Shh, everything's okay. You're going to be just fine."

"Hold me. Don't let go. Please...don't leave me alone."

"I'm here. I'll stay with you as long as you want me to." As he said the words, he went over what Darvi had told him. So, that was the basis of her anguish—guilt over a miscarriage. Two years of self-imposed hell, living with blame over something in which she had no culpability. An accident that had been the result of one man's cruel and cold manipulation.

Darvi gradually quieted. She seemed to be calmer now and yet never more vulnerable, so in need of someone.

He drew in a calming breath.

So in need of him.

Chapter Six

Darvi woke with a start. Her gaze darted around the room as she tried to collect her thoughts and get her bearings. Rance was there, on the couch with her. His arms enveloped her in a warm, protective cocoon. She looked at him, wariness and uncertainty churning inside her. Did he feel disgust? Did he now find her beneath contempt?

He brushed a loose tendril of hair from her cheek, then kissed her forehead. "Are you okay?"

Relief flooded through her as she heard what she perceived to be his reassurance and acceptance. "This is the second time in two days I've fallen asleep on my couch in your arms. I promise not to make a habit of this."

"There's no reason for you to apologize. Now, back to my question. Are you okay?"

Darvi rested her head against his chest, her voice quiet but firm. "You're treating me like some fragile little flower." She raised her head so she could look up at his face. "Is that the way you're going to talk to me from now on? Every time you see me, you're going to feel obligated to ask me if I'm okay? I know I've been acting like an emotional basket case, but I'm not one. Really, I'm not."

He smiled. "Just humor me this one last time. Are you okay?"

"Yes, I think so." Her brow furrowed as a sense of relief washed over her. "Yes, I'm okay." She offered a tentative bit of a smile. "This time, I really mean it."

She did feel better, much better. She had been so frightened the entire time she was telling Rance what happened. Fearful that he would be disgusted with her, appalled at the way she had allowed herself to be so callously manipulated and used. But he didn't seem to be either one. He did not view her with hard eyes. His touch had not turned cold. Had the unprecedented chance she had taken in trusting him with her most closely guarded and painful secret actually paid off? For the first time since that horrible night, she had put her vulnerability on the line, had allowed someone to see it. She felt better, lighter in spirit with each passing minute.

Rance had literally forced her to talk about it. He had reached deep inside her, to her most hidden vault where she had locked away her darkest secret, and yanked it out into the open. And he had been right. Shared in the harsh light of reality, it did not seem as totally overwhelming as it once had. It had been a long time since she felt this comfortable and relaxed. A long time since she felt this safe, secure and—well, so cared for.

Rance took in the vulnerability in her beautiful emerald eyes. He was fully aware of the way she clung to him, how she had curled her legs under her as she sat cradled in his arms. The fullness of her firm breasts pressed against him.

The full impact of his errant thoughts suddenly hit him. Darvi had just been through hell, a gut-wrenching experience in which he had pushed and badgered her, forcing her to bare her soul, exposing her darkest and most painful secret.

And what is it you're doing, you insensitive ass? You're checking out her body while entertaining thoughts of sex. Of course, you want her.

Rance's thoughts softened as he allowed his own carefully protected feelings to skirt the surface. He had wanted her from the moment he first saw those angry flashing green eyes and that copper hair glistening in the morning sun when he had confronted her on the street. From the first time he had felt the warmth of her touch as they shook hands when they were introduced at the inn. From the moment he had seen her smile and heard her laugh.

He knew all too well how vulnerable she was right now, how much she wanted and needed the closeness of a caring person. But, if he betrayed the tenuous trust she had placed in him, he would be no better than that bastard Jerry Peterson. No, he would wait. They would make love because they both wanted the same thing, not because he caught her in a moment of weakness or taken advantage of her vulnerability.

He knew something else, too, something much deeper. He cared about Darvi Stanton more than he had any other woman. He would go to any lengths to protect her, to keep her from being hurt again, even if it stirred up his own fears and conflicts.

If—there was no *if* about it. His own fears and conflicts were already solidly involved. The next couple of hours were spent in silence until the last light of day filtered softly through the windows as the air turned chilly. She had remained motionless for the past hour. He did not know whether she was awake or asleep. He slowly shifted his position. One arm was numb, and his leg had started to cramp due to the uncomfortable posture he had maintained in an attempt to keep from disturbing her.

As soon as he moved, she sat up. He immediately grabbed her hand. "I didn't mean to wake you. It's just that—" He grinned sheepishly at her. "You've cut off my circulation. I'm losing use of some vital body parts."

Darvi allowed a shy smile to curl her lips. "Nothing too vital, I hope." A heated flush spread across her cheeks as her own words embarrassed her.

"Nothing that will prevent me from doing this." He took her face in his hands and lowered his mouth to hers. His kiss was gentle. No heated passion. Just the softness of tender care and concern.

She ran her fingers across his cheek, placed the palm of her hand along the side of his face, and drew back until she could look into his eyes. She searched, not exactly sure what she hoped to find. Her gaze lingered on the confusion in his eyes.

"Darvi, what is it? What's the matter?"

She opened her mouth to speak, but no words came out. Indecision darted through her. She tried again. "Rance...would you stay with me tonight?"

First stunned, followed by a lingering surprise, and finally, a warm glow of pleasure slowly spread across his face. "You want me to spend the night with you—here? *All* night?"

"That's not what I mean." She shyly lowered her eyelids, then recaptured his gaze. "It's just that I don't want to be alone tonight." Her eyes started to mist. "Please, stay with me." She offered him the tiniest of smiles. "I've been through a lot today."

Rance searched her eyes. Her panic had disappeared, and in its stead, he saw fear, but it was different from the fear that had been there earlier. This was not fear born of a dark secret. It was a fear more akin to anxiety that someone would experience when starting down an unknown path toward an unknown destination.

"Of course. I'll stay with you as long as you want me to." He took her hand in his. "You don't have any reason to be afraid of what might happen. You'll be safe with me…honest."

"I know." She brushed her lips against his. "I trust you."

****

Rance looked at the clock by Darvi's bed. Midnight, and he was still wide-awake. He glanced at her sleeping peacefully in his arms. There had been a bit of awkwardness at bedtime. He hadn't wanted to presume he would be spending the night in her bed rather than on the couch. He had wondered whether he should leave his clothes on, strip to his briefs, or sleep in the nude as he usually did at home.

He had not been able to put it off any longer, so he finally worked up the courage to just be direct and ask her. "Where do you want me to sleep?" The question had genuinely embarrassed him.

She had hesitated for an uncertain moment, then taken his hand in hers. "Come sleep with me. If you sleep out here on the couch, you might as well be home." As she had led him into her bedroom, a tremor of panic grabbed him.

Darvi stirred, drawing Rance's attention back to the present. Her face momentarily contorted into a mask of anguish then softened as she seemed to relax. She appeared to be sound asleep. He closed his eyes and willed himself to go to sleep. He finally drifted off into darkness.

****

The predawn light filtered through the window. Darvi lay quietly in bed, the light just strong enough for her to make out Rance's handsome features. She studied his face as she reached out to trace his jaw with her fingers. Her gaze wandered over his broad shoulders, strong arms, and muscular chest.

One of his arms rested under her body and around her shoulder where it had been all night. She felt so secure in his embrace. It had been a long time since she felt this relaxed and comfortable. A long time since she felt this safe, secure, and cared for. She watched him sleep. No one had ever shown as much concern for her as he had last night. Not even her own family.

Darvi's mother had died when she was only three years old. Her father had been at a loss about raising a little girl. He had coped with the situation by keeping his distance. As a result, he had seemed remote and untouchable for her entire life, barely more than a stranger.

She had talked briefly with the psychologist and the social worker at the hospital following her miscarriage. It had done nothing to erase her feelings of blame and guilt. However, it had given her a little insight into the dynamic of Jerry as a father figure and how that had resulted in a drive to please him so he would care about her, something she had never been able to accomplish with her father when she was a child. Even though she believed her father loved her, their relationship had never been what she could call comfortable.

Rance turned over on his side, interrupting her reflections. He placed his other arm across her waist and nuzzled his face against the side of her breast. Darvi's nipples puckered at the warmth of his breath through the fabric of her pajama top.

She knew he was asleep and not intentionally trying to take advantage of her, but the feel of his body pressed against hers excited her senses. Her skin tingled, and her breathing quickened. She wanted to touch him, run her fingertips across his chest. Giving conscious thought to her desires embarrassed her. She refused to dwell on the other things she wanted to do to him. And most certainly *with* him.

A quick note of caution invaded her thoughts. Was she projecting more on the situation than she should? Once again allowing herself to be drawn in without clearly understanding the rules of the *game*? Or more specifically, Rance's rules of this particular game? She closed her eyes and tried to center herself. Whatever was going to happen, she needed to be constantly aware of the changing parameters.

Rance gradually became cognizant of being awake. He didn't move, did not open his eyes. He attempted to sort out everything in his mind—his current surroundings, what happened last night, and what was going on around him now. He felt comfortable and warm in bed with her, even with the hands-off mode he had silently agreed to honor. A hazy thought drifted through his sleep-clogged mind about wanting to spend the rest of his life just like this.

The feel of her fingers running lightly across his shoulder broke his moment of reverie. He remained still, reveling in the sensations her delicate touch aroused in him. He now realized just how close his face—his mouth—was to her breast. He felt the rise and fall of her breathing. He stirred, stretched out his tall frame, tightened his arms around her, and drew her closer.

His body seemed to be functioning separately from his conscious control. His mouth sought out the taut nipple that protruded against the soft material of her pajama top. He gently took the nipple into his mouth, the fabric along with it. His hand moved from her waist over the fabric of her pajamas and up her rib cage toward her other breast.

Darvi let out a small gasp as his mouth closed over the delicate peak. She dug her fingers into his shoulder as she arched her back, forcing her breast more fully against his mouth.

Rance jerked upright in a state of shock. "Darvi..." He tugged at the wet fabric, pulling it away from where it clung to her hardened nipple. "I'm sorry—I didn't mean for that to happen."

He quickly released her from his arms, running his fingers nervously through his tousled hair as he tried to collect his composure. He swung his long legs around and sat on the edge of the bed as he grabbed his jeans from the floor. After hastily pulling them on, he turned back to her. With trembling hands, he reached down and pulled the covers up to her neck and tucked them in along her shoulders.

He looked nervously into her eyes. "You trusted me, and I just violated that trust. I didn't mean to. It wasn't my intention, but that doesn't change the fact that it happened." His brow furrowed as he tightened his grip on the blankets. "I'm so sorry. Please forgive me."

She reached her arm out from under the covers and placed her hand on his cheek. Her eyes radiated a softness, not frightened as they had been in the past.

"There's nothing to forgive." Her voice was quiet yet warm and open. She moved her hand along the side of his neck and rested it gently against his chest. "You asked me to trust—demanded I trust—and finally forced me to trust you. I'm the one who insisted you stay. You've done nothing to betray that trust."

They locked gazes. A jolt of intense feeling passed between them. Maybe Darvi felt safe, but Rance found himself rapidly sinking into panic. He tentatively encircled her in his arms and drew her up against his body. She returned his embrace.

While slowly pulling out of Rance's arms, she glanced at the clock. "We have a meeting with George tomorrow morning at the inn so he can approve my designs, and I'm not quite ready for it." She turned to look at him. Once again she placed her hand on his cheek, her fingers barely touching his skin. An uninvited ripple of desire darted through him. "Thank you for staying with me last night. It meant a lot to know I wasn't alone."

She studied him, as if turning some thoughts over in her mind. She finally formulated her words. "For two years now, I've had a recurring nightmare. Whenever anything or anyone got close enough to me that I felt emotionally threatened, I'd be plagued with this nightmare until I got rid of whatever...or whoever...frightened me. It's always the same. I'm being chased by a dark, shadowy figure. I keep running as fast as I can, but I can't get away. It's always right behind me, reaching out, almost able to grab me. That's when I wake up, terrified, with my heart pounding in my chest."

Her nightmare. He had witnessed it the evening after

the softball game, when she had fallen asleep in his arms on the couch. He swallowed, trying to lessen the lump in his throat. He couldn't identify the exact emotion coursing through his veins nor did he understand what it meant.

"Last night the nightmare started again." Rance pulled her to him. Her body trembled in his arms. "I ran the way I always do, trying to escape the danger. Then I gathered my determination and decided to stand my ground. I stopped and turned to confront the demon chasing me…my nemesis. The shadowy figure moved into the light. To my shock—" A hard shudder engulfed her as she took a deep breath. "—the demon was me. I had been my own mysterious tormenter in my recurring nightmare. Everything instantly jumped into crystal clarity—I had been terrorizing myself for two years. Punishing myself for what I believed was my fault. In my mind, I heard your voice telling me it wasn't my fault. As soon as I accepted that, everything in the nightmare instantly vanished in a puff of smoke as if it had never happened."

She furrowed her brow for a moment. "I hope I'm interpreting it correctly, that my fears have emerged from the darkness of that closet you mentioned, so the harsh light of reality could permanently banish them along with my nightmare." Her words were more of a reflection than a statement.

She leaned her face toward him and lightly brushed her lips against his. "That's why I wanted you to stay with me, why I didn't want to be alone. I was afraid the nightmare would return"—she allowed a shy smile—"in spite of everything you put me through." Her expression turned serious, her manner tentative. "I hope it wasn't too much of an inconvenience for you."

Rance took her hand in his, lifted it to his lips, and kissed her palm. "It was not an inconvenience, not at all."

He made coffee and Darvi set out some fresh fruit and breakfast rolls. About an hour passed before he finally took his leave, both agreeing that they needed to get to work.

Darvi finished the last of the watercolor renditions of her designs. Even though George had not officially approved them, she would go ahead and start on the full-size cartoons and the cutline tracings. She wanted to be ready to start on the actual windows as soon as possible. She had already sorted through the different pieces of colored glass she had on hand and made a list of supplies she needed to order from Amy.

Her mind kept wandering back to Rance. He had reluctantly left her studio well after sunrise. As he said when he left, Sandy Cove was a small, close-knit town. By noon, everyone would know his car had been at her studio all night.

She tried to clear the distracting thoughts from her head and return to her work but without any success. Her spirits soared. It had been a long time since she felt so light and free. He had lifted her from the depths of fear and terror and raised her to a new level of self-confidence and strength. She didn't have any delusions about whether *all* her fear and guilt had suddenly been swept away, but her breakthrough represented a great start. She hadn't experienced such a feeling of optimism in a long time—if ever.

She leaned back in her chair, closed her eyes, and allowed a smile to curl the corners of her mouth. Her skin tingled and her breathing quickened as she recalled

Rance's warm mouth capturing her taut nipple through the fabric of her pajama top. A contented sigh escaped her lips as the sensations washed over her. No question in her mind, no confusion in her thoughts—they would definitely make love. And soon.

Rance had driven straight home after leaving Darvi's studio that morning. He'd grabbed a quick shower, shaved, and put on clean clothes. He went immediately to his workshop. Unlike Darvi, he was ready for the meeting with George. He had his patterns set and had already placed an order with Frank for the specific types of wood he needed. As soon as it arrived, Bobby could start cutting the larger pieces of the patterns. Rance had the cut list and layout ready for him. When satisfied everything was in order, he headed to the construction site to check in with Bill Jenkins and get a status report.

As he drove, he let his mind drift. An image burned into his memory—the way Darvi had looked while standing at the door of her studio when they had exchanged their first kiss, what he hoped would be the first of many such passionate kisses. Then his mind wandered to that morning in her bed. He smiled as he recalled the sensation of her taut nipple in his mouth.

Rance, ol' boy, you have all the will power of...well, I don't know of what, but you behaved like a real ass.

As he pulled into the parking lot at the inn, confusion filled his thoughts. Exactly what type of relationship did he have with Darvi? Or, more importantly, could it really be called the beginning of a true relationship? An emotional melding? And if so, was it something he would be able to accept and handle?

Panic welled inside him as he thought about what

she had confessed—about her pregnancy and the final confrontation with Jerry Peterson that had ended with her miscarriage. Her story had hit an extremely vulnerable spot inside him, a spot he had carefully protected from all outside influences for the past ten years. And now, he had allowed himself to feel again, a reality that truly frightened him. He shoved down the trepidation that tried to establish a foothold.

Darvi was special to him. He had literally forced her into a highly emotional angst-ridden confession. He could not turn his back on the emotional connection growing between them, no matter how much it scared him. And he definitely could not turn his back on the emotional upheaval that confession had created for her—a confession he had forced from her.

****

Darvi's clock chimed five times. She declared it the end of her workday, time to clean up her studio. She had everything ready for the meeting with George at ten o'clock in the morning and had gotten a good start on the next phase of the windows. She looked at the material spread out in front of her, pleased with what she saw. Some of the best work she had ever done. She felt good about this project. Very confident. Once George approved the sketches and color schemes, the creative effort would give way to the work of physically constructing the windows.

She flipped on the television to catch the news as she prepared something to eat. The weather forecast did not sound good. The unseasonably warm, sunny days they had been enjoying were about to come to an end. A series of storms spread out across the Pacific Ocean and would be coming onshore one right after the other. It looked as if they were in for at least a month of cold, rainy weather.

After dinner she did the dishes, took a bath, then slipped into a robe. She arranged the pillows on top of her bed in a comfortable manner so she could sit up and read for a while. She had just turned the radio to a soft music station and settled in with her book when the doorbell intruded.

She padded barefoot to the front door, turned on the porch light, and looked through the peephole. The sight of Rance standing on the other side both surprised and pleased her. After unhooking the night latch, she opened the door and let him in.

"Before tomorrow's meeting we should do a last-minute comparison of our—" Rance stopped in midsentence as his eyes adjusted to the dim light.

The green silk robe hugged Darvi's curves. The hem fell halfway down her thighs. His gaze followed down her long, sleek legs and back up to where the front of the robe parted slightly, exposing the curve of her breast.

The delicate scent of her bath oil wafted across the open space between them, filling him with a sense of urgency. The carrying case slipped from his hand, hitting the floor with a loud thud.

Chapter Seven

Rance reached out an unsteady hand and took the pins from Darvi's hair, watching as the copper tresses cascaded over her shoulders. His trembling hands cupped her face as he looked longingly into the emerald depths of her beautiful eyes. Everything that had shown in her eyes before—fear, anger, wariness, uncertainty—had disappeared. Instead, the confidence, determination, and a haunting sensuality almost knocked him back on his heels. He lowered his mouth to hers as he enfolded her in his arms. His legitimate reason for being at her studio—wanting to do a last-minute check before their meeting the next morning—vanished from reality in a flash of heated desire.

She melted in his embrace as his mouth captured hers. Their tongues danced and twined in the moist darkness. Their breathing turned labored. He held her close. His hands moved across her back then dropped to her firm, round bottom. The silky fabric of her robe hiked up higher and higher with each foray of his hands.

He felt himself slipping beyond the point of no return. He wanted her, wanted her more than he was willing to admit, more than he had ever wanted anyone. His husky voice managed a few words between kisses. "You once told me…if you wanted me to kiss you…you'd let me know. Since we've already moved beyond that…so does that now apply…to making love?

Do I assume it's okay? Should I ask?"

"If you don't make love to me right now—" she said, her words labored, her tone teasing, "I'll never speak to you again."

He pulled his face back from hers, a mischievous grin playing at the corners of his mouth. "That will never do. We need to be on speaking terms to finish the inn project. Besides, I can't stand the silent treatment. So…I guess I have no choice other than to comply."

He turned the bolt on the front door to secure the lock, took her hand in his, and led her toward her bedroom at the back of the studio. Halfway across the room he stopped short, whirled around, and placed his hands on her shoulders. Intense concern blanketed his features. "Darvi, I wasn't prepared for this. I didn't come here assuming we'd end up in bed. I don't have anything with me. Are you on birth control? Is it okay? Do I need to run home and get—"

She put her fingers to his lips. Her voice contained just a hint of sadness. "It's…that won't be necessary."

Rance took her hand again. He noted the touch of sadness but didn't know exactly how to interpret it. "Is something wrong?" A shiver of apprehension shot through his body. "Are…are you having second thoughts? Have you changed your mind? Is it something else?"

"No, that's not…after the accident and my miscarriage, the doctor said I couldn't have any more children. I…" She offered a shy smile. "I'm not having second thoughts and haven't changed my mind. I'm…" She searched his face for something, then lowered her gaze to the floor. She drew in a deep breath and slowly exhaled. "I haven't been with anyone since then."

He squeezed her hand, and they continued on through the studio. As they entered her bedroom, once again the aura of the setting engulfed him. The fragrances, the muted colors, the soft textures—they all played on his senses. He felt himself slipping into another time and place, losing himself to her soft sensuality.

As he pulled her body against his, he captured her mouth with a burning need. Her hands moved up under his sweater and across his chest. Her touch sent tingling sensations across his skin. She splayed her fingers, covering as much of his bare skin at one time as possible.

Darvi's senses reeled. They would make love because of a mutual attraction and desire, not because she needed to please him or wanted his approval. She had never felt so excited…so alive…so desirable…so free… Words deserted her as she gave herself over to the fire Rance lit inside her. The last word to flit consciously through her mind? *Love*. She wasn't sure where the word came from, but it settled over her, wrapping her in a warm cocoon.

Desire surged through her as she moved her hands across his skin, pausing to tug at his sweater. As soon as he released her from his embrace, she pulled his sweater off over his head and dropped it to the floor.

Rance nibbled at her mouth, tasted the sweetness of her lips, caressed her cheek, and the curve of her neck. He wanted to consume her completely, totally, wholly. But, before he got to that point of no return, he made one final stab at being sensible. That glimpse of sadness in her eyes bothered him, lingering in his mind.

"Are you sure? Are you really sure?" His erratic breathing gave his voice a husky sound.

"I'm very sure," she murmured in a voice so filled with desire he almost melted on the spot.

Slowly, almost like some ancient ritual of seduction, they undressed each other. He kicked off his shoes as he untied the sash around her waist. Her robe parted as the sash fell to the floor. A sensual moan escaped his throat as her nude body met his gaze. He slipped his hands inside her robe, reveling in the silky smoothness of her skin. His gentle touch expertly danced across her body. His hands trailed over her hips, up her rib cage, across her back, down to her bottom, and back up to her waist.

She unsnapped his jeans and lowered the zipper, his arousal evident as her fingers brushed over his briefs. The sensual feel of her touch elicited a gasp from him. She tugged his jeans past his hips. He recaptured her mouth as his hands moved up her rib cage, then he paused at her firm breasts. He cupped them, her hardened nipples pressing into his palms, and all the while, his tongue explored and tasted the textures of her mouth. He slid his hands up over her smooth shoulders then slowly removed her robe, allowing it to fall on the floor. After he laid her back across the bed, he doffed the rest of his clothes in one quick motion.

She stretched out her body, then reached her arms up to Rance, beckoning him to join her. He hesitated a moment, his gaze drinking in her delectable curves. The flowing tresses framed her face and fanned out over the pillow where she rested her head, just as he had envisioned it on numerous occasions. Her eyes sparkled with passion as she looked up at him, her slightly parted lips still wet and swollen from the feverish kisses they had shared. The sight mesmerized him. His heart beat increased. His breath came faster.

Rance sank onto the bed, pulling her to him. "You're very beautiful. Not only to look at and touch, but to be with." He brushed his lips across her face—her cheeks, her forehead, the tip of her nose—in an attempt to stop the words he feared he might not be able to control. "Tell me what you would like, what excites you, how I can please you."

Darvi's thoughts whirled. No one had ever asked her that before. No one had ever put her wants and needs ahead of their own. She rubbed her bare leg against Rance's as her long fingers trailed up and down his back.

"How did I ever get so lucky to be here with you?" she murmured in his ear and melted into his tender ministrations.

He kissed the side of her neck, her throat, her shoulders. "I'm the one who's lucky."

He cupped one breast as he sought out her other breast with his mouth. He captured the delicate peak between his lips and gently sucked, his tongue flicking across the pebbled texture.

A moan of delight escaped her lips as she arched her back, exerting more pressure against his sensual mouth. She stroked his body with her hands, his skin hot to the touch as she trailed her fingers across his hard, flat belly.

Rance quickly moved to her other breast. His hands stroked the smooth skin of her inner thighs. A delicious shudder shot through her body and settled low in the heated center of her femininity. His fingers twirled through the downy softness between her thighs, then slowly slipped through the moist folds of her sex.

He cut off her whimper of delight when he brought his mouth down hard on hers, his labored breathing matching her own. She had never before felt the level of excitement he aroused in her, experienced such all-consuming passion. They were caught up in an inferno. Everywhere he touched her compounded the heat.

Rance trailed hot kisses across her body—the soft skin of the valley between her breasts, her smooth stomach. "I want to know all of you, touch you, taste you…"

Darvi's entire body quivered in sweet anticipation. It had been a long time since her last sexual encounter. Two years of stored up passion raced through her veins. With trembling fingers, she reached for his hardened arousal. His quick intake of breath reached her ears, followed by his moan of pure pleasure.

He slowly rolled her over on top of him. "You're so exquisite," he said, his voice husky in her ear, "so incredible."

He lifted her hips and brought her down on his erection, penetrating the velvety, moist heat of her body as he filled her with his hardness.

Darvi's head jerked back, and her eyes squeezed shut. The searing sensations almost took her senses away as she trembled with anticipation. "Rance…oh, Rance—"

His mouth cut off her words as he rolled her onto her back, careful not to break the tangible connection between them. His hips moved in a slow, even rhythm as he threaded his fingers through her long hair.

She moved in harmony with his strokes. They each experienced the torrid sensations building, piling one on top of the other, until they were lost in the excitement of heated passion with no holding back.

The convulsions started deep inside Darvi and spread until she could no longer contain them. He had taken her beyond anything she had ever experienced. She had never before known the level of ecstasy to match that moment. So much more than mere sex. She didn't know how to describe what she felt both physical and emotional…the overall sensation surging through her body.

Rance threw his head back as a growl of intense pleasure clawed its way out of his throat. His body shuddered, accompanied by deep spasms, as he buried his face in her copper tresses and held her tightly in his embrace.

A quiet euphoria settled over them as they descended from the heights. She cuddled against his damp chest. His breathing returned to normal, as did hers. Neither seemed able to speak—nor for that matter, wanted to. Words were unnecessary. They basked in the warmth of their union, enjoying the closeness of the moment. He smoothed back a loose tendril of hair clinging to her moist cheek as he pressed his lips against her forehead.

"Rance…" Darvi lifted her head from his chest.

"Shh. Whatever it is, don't confound me with mere words. I can't think straight." He stroked her hair as he looked into her upturned face. "You have me completely befuddled."

He brushed his lips against hers, the kiss light, but the meaning deep. A contented sigh escaped her lips. She closed her eyes as she again snuggled against him.

His body may have been at rest, but not his mind. He had never felt so at one with another person in his life. He wanted to stay in her bed forever. And those thoughts bothered him. No, they more than bothered him. They terrified him, even more than he had first realized. He knew at that moment he had been falling in love with Darvi from the first time he had laid eyes on her, before he even knew who she was. The realization should have excited him, should have warmed the cold place that had lived inside him all these years.

The reality, however, presented quite the divergent problem. Panic screamed in his head, telling him to get out while he could. He had not been looking for a relationship, had purposely avoided anything that approached a commitment. He had been perfectly satisfied with his life when this woman had suddenly became entwined with his daily existence.

What to do…what to do.

He *knew* what he wanted to do, what he wanted to say to her. He glanced at her nestled in his arms, then placed his cheek against her head as he let out a sigh. "What are we going to do about this? About us?"

Darvi opened her eyes, raised her head, and looked at him. "Do about this? What do you mean by *do about this*?" Her expression mirrored her confusion over his statement. "Is something wrong?"

He studied her for a long moment. "This wasn't my intention when I came here tonight—to end up in bed with you."

Uncertainty emanated from her green eyes. "I don't understand, Rance." An unmistakable timbre of hurt had entered her voice. "Are you saying you're sorry we made love? That you really didn't want to?" Panic widened her eyes. "That I somehow coerced you into this for my own ulterior motives?"

He shifted his weight to his side and propped himself up on his elbow, then took her face in his hands as he looked into her eyes. Things were moving too fast.

Shawna Delacorte

He didn't know how Darvi felt, but he wasn't anywhere close to being ready for a personal commitment. "No, that's not what I meant. I just wanted to make sure you were comfortable with what happened tonight, that's all. That you didn't have any regrets."

Not what he wanted to say, but it would have to do.

"No, no regrets at all." She eyed him cautiously. "How about you? You seem reticent, somehow bothered. Are you experiencing some regrets?"

"Of course not." Rance settled back into the softness of the bed, pulling her with him. She was everything he wanted, everything he needed. Did he dare consider some type of limited commitment? To visualize his future in entirely different terms—as a future that would include someone special? Someone named Darvi Stanton? But what did *limited commitment* even mean? It sounded temporary, not the permanent relationship he had secretly yearned for even if he refused to acknowledge the reality. So many questions without any answers.

The sensation of her fingers tickling across his bare thigh drove all thoughts from his mind—all except one. He captured her taut nipple in the warmth of his mouth as he gently stroked the smooth skin of her inner thigh.

Darvi sighed as she ran her fingers through his thick, sandy-colored hair. She had never felt so satisfied, so complete, so totally head over heels in love as she did at that moment. "Mmm. You do such marvelous things to me. You make me feel so desirable and sexy."

Sensual stirrings moved provocatively through her body, creating a new urgency.

****

The first gray streaks of daylight challenged the

night sky. Even in the dim predawn light, Darvi could see through the window to the cloud cover that threatened rain. She snuggled closer to Rance as she pulled the covers up around their shoulders.

He slept peacefully, his arms still around her. She studied his handsome features, lightly ran her fingertips across the whiskers that stubbled his face, smoothed his tousled hair from his forehead. It had been quite a night. They had made love two more times, and it had transcended anything she had ever experienced.

Even now, it seemed like a fantasy. She feared she would wake up and find it had all been a dream. She watched as he stirred, stretched, and opened his eyes. As soon as he focused on her, he smiled and pulled her close. She felt so warm and safe in his arms. Life truly moved in mysterious ways. For the first time, she believed life could be wonderful—that she could look forward to what the future held.

"Good morning." Rance's voice sounded thick with sleep. He reached out and touched her cheek, as if making sure she was really there. "Did you sleep well?"

"I've never slept better in my life. How about you?"

"Perfect." He rolled over on top of her, nuzzling the side of her neck before burying his face in her hair. He ran his fingers along the length of her body and stroked her hair as he held her in his arms. "I hate to break the mood by changing the subject, but I have a carrying case somewhere in your studio. I wanted to do a last-minute check before today's meeting with George."

Darvi beamed at him as an impish grin twitched at the corners of her mouth. "Correct me if I'm wrong, but didn't we do a fairly in-depth check of another kind last night?"

"That we did." Rance chuckled. "But nothing I intend to share with George."

She reluctantly withdrew from his embrace. "Our meeting is at ten o'clock. We'd better do something about getting ready for it. I'll go start the coffee, then I want to grab a quick shower."

A lustful expression danced across his face. "If you don't mind, I'll use your shower while you're putting on the coffee." He tilted his head and raised a questioning eyebrow. "Then perhaps I can talk you into joining me there?"

She brushed her fingers across his chest as she slipped out of bed and grabbed her robe from the floor where it had fallen the night before. "Perhaps you can…" She gazed into his eyes, the love she felt welling inside her. "Change that *perhaps* to a *definitely*." She pulled on the silk robe and headed for the kitchen.

Rance's smoldering gaze followed her. As much as he wanted to stay with her, just the two of them hidden away from the world, he knew they needed to return their attention to work. If George approved Darvi's preliminary presentation, they would have a couple of busy months. Besides, he wanted to avoid any conversation with Darvi that might center on what path their personal future should take. The thought still left him very uneasy, uncertain, and totally confused.

Their shower together ended up being only a shower. Even though they each experienced continuing sensual desires, the needs of the outside world took precedence. They shared a quick breakfast, then Rance hurried home to prepare for their meeting with George.

Darvi watched him drive away, her body still tingling from the intensity of last night's lovemaking.

She allowed a moment of reflection about what the future might hold, then turned her attention to gathering her materials and dressing for work.

****

A cold wind whipped through Darvi as she darted across the parking lot toward the construction trailer office at the inn. She looked up at the threatening sky. It would surely be raining within the hour. As she approached the door to the trailer, it swung open, and Bill Jenkins emerged.

"Good morning, Darvi." He motioned back over his shoulder. "George is inside." He held the door for her then hurried toward the inn.

"Darvi, good morning." George's cheery hello and good-natured smile greeted her as she stepped inside the office.

"Good morning. It looks like it's going to pour any minute." She set her portfolio case and large shoulder bag on the floor.

George helped her off with her jacket. "This is the kind of day that calls for a fire in the lobby fireplace. Unfortunately, the only wood we have is what the construction crew needs. If we value our existence, we'd better leave it alone." George looked out the window to the parking lot. "Ah, here comes Rance. Now, we can get started."

A cold gust of wind swept through the trailer as Rance opened the door. "Whew, there's a major storm brewing out there. I think we're really in for it."

Rance set his case next to Darvi's as he extended his hand to George. "Good morning. Nice to see you again." After the two men shook hands, Rance immediately turned his attention to Darvi. His expression softened, his eyes taking in her every nuance. He reached out, briefly touched his fingertips to her cheek then quickly withdrew his hand. "Good morning, Darvi."

George beamed like a proud father. "Well, I see you two are getting along much better than you were when we got together three weeks ago."

She lowered her eyelids as the blush spread across her cheeks. Rance shot her an endearing look then returned his attention to George, his manner all business. "Yes, I think her ideas will definitely enhance the overall aesthetics of this project. Darvi is a very talented artist. I don't think there will be any problems completing the work on time."

George smiled as he nodded his head knowingly. "Of course."

For the next three hours, they went through the inn room by room as Darvi showed George the watercolor paintings of the proposed windows and presented her color schemes and room themes. Rance gave George copies of the inlaid wood patterns for the doors.

When they reached the corner suites, she produced drawings for three windows making up one scene that wrapped around the corner of the lower-level living room and two windows for the corner of the upper-level bedroom. The new idea had occurred to her the previous morning, and she had worked hard on it all day long.

"Where did that come from?" Rance's voice carried a less than cordial tone as he interrupted her presentation. "You didn't run that idea by me."

Her surprise at his unexpected comments immediately transformed into defensiveness as she glared at him. "I didn't realize I was required to have my creativity pre-approved by you. Everything that corresponds with your doors is still present in the new windows, so you won't need to make any changes in your work."

He stretched to his full six-foot one-inch, his body language issuing his challenge and displeasure as much as his words. "As the building contractor, I have window dimensions to consider as does the architect." He gestured toward George. "Things such as placement, revised blueprints, structural considerations. You knew that."

"The idea just occurred to me yesterday morning." She spat out the words. "I would have apprised you of the changes last night after I finished the watercolor renderings if—"

She caught herself in time before blurting out the circumstances of their involvement in front of George. Shifting emotions darted through his eyes as his expression softened.

"Now, now. I thought you two had signed a peace treaty." George addressed his next comments to Rance. "I like the idea. There won't be any problem changing the blueprints to accommodate the new windows, especially since they aren't unusual shapes or sizes. I trust there won't be any problems on the construction side?"

"No...of course not."

"Good. Then that's settled. There is no problem."

They left the inn and returned to the construction trailer. George signed off on the work presented to him. "I'm very impressed. We'll proceed exactly as you've outlined. I don't have a single change."

George shook hands with Darvi then Rance. He directed his comments to Rance. "Well, I guess that does it. I'll check with you in a couple of weeks to get an update on the construction. Meanwhile, any questions or problems, give me a call at my Portland office."

The three of them exchanged goodbyes. Darvi and Rance watched as George left the trailer and hurried to his car. Large raindrops splattered on the ground as the sky turned even darker. Rance reached out, took Darvi's hand, and gave it a little squeeze as he continued to stare out the window. "It looks like you have your work cut out for you. I don't know a whole lot about making stained-glass windows, but I do know that it'll take you a lot longer than it will for me to do the doors. Especially since you have many more windows to do. I have only one door per room. Besides, I have Bobby helping me."

She jerked her hand from his grasp, surprised at his about-face in attitude. One minute he had been challenging her and the next minute he was intimately holding her hand as if nothing adverse had happened.

"What the hell was all that about?" Her voice clearly conveyed her displeasure with him. "How dare you take me to task like that and in front of George."

His temper flared to match hers. "How dare you let me find out about your changes by hearing them when you present them to George. I'm the contractor. I have to maintain control over this project. I can't do it if the people working for me—"

"Working *for you?*" Her eyes widened in shock. She stood with her hands on her hips, as she glared at him. "I was hired by George and am being paid directly by him, not you. And, I might add, over your many loud and adamant objections to him hiring me."

The clash of words and wills bordered on being out of hand. They both knew they had lots of work to do and a tight schedule. Neither of them could afford this type of distraction. Their working relationship had already taken a distinct turn from strictly business to very personal, which presented distraction enough. And now, even that personal involvement had taken a sharp turn.

An image popped into Rance's consciousness, that of Darvi stretched out across the bed with her arms raised toward him, beckoning him to join her there.

"All right…working *with* me." His husky voice was not at all in keeping with the fiery words they had exchanged moments earlier.

Without warning, he grabbed her wrist and pulled her into his arms. His mouth came down hard against hers as he infused her with all the passion flowing inside him, all the passion they had shared the previous night.

As angry as he made her, Darvi could not resist the sensuality of the man. She melted into his embrace, willingly accepting his tongue as it probed the dark recesses of her mouth. Any lingering outrage vanished in a flash of heated desire.

He flicked his tongue across her lower lip then spoke. "I don't suppose we can do this for the rest of the day. Or maybe at least through lunch?"

Chapter Eight

Their agreement to start work right after lunch lasted only a few minutes. The increasing passion that existed between them had quickly overshadowed good intentions. Rance kissed Darvi's bare shoulder as he trailed his fingers across her hip. He paused, his brow knitting into a frown as he felt the raised scar…the visible reminder of the night her torment began. He wrapped his arms around her as they shared a quiet moment following their lovemaking.

"Bill Jenkins has things under control and is actually ahead of schedule in some areas which allows me some extra free time. As I said earlier, I don't know very much about making stained-glass windows, but I'm a pretty quick study. Is there anything I can do to help you?"

She rested her head against his chest and nestled into his embrace, the warmth of her body radiating to him. "I can't think of anything. I'm organized and have most of my materials on hand. Unless some unexpected setback comes along, I don't anticipate any problems with the schedule."

He closed his eyes as he allowed the sensations of touch and smell to wash over him—the feel of her skin, her long red hair, and the textures of the lace and soft fabrics surrounding them as they lay in her canopied bed. The combined fragrances of the potpourri and sachets mingled with the scents of the various bath oils in the bathroom.

And all of it blending with the aroma of sex clinging to their skin.

Evening drifted into night as they continued to hold each other, reveling in the closeness. They talked, exchanging the details of their lives. He wanted to know everything about her, everything down to her favorite toy as a child.

"You know all about me, including my limited and unlucky history with men. What about you?" She cautiously tendered the words. "Have you ever been married? Do you have any children?"

Even though he had pushed her, dug into her past, refused to let her off the hook for answering his questions, it almost appeared as if she believed she had somehow invaded his privacy by wanting the same information from him.

He hesitated a moment, not sure quite what to say. She posed a fair question, especially in light of the way he had badgered her. After a moment of contemplation, he tried his best to answer her questions as honestly as he could.

"I was married once for seven horrible months. Joan and I had been casually dating for about three months when she informed me she was pregnant and I was the father." He hesitated again, the bitter memories hard for him to verbalize. "I thought I had taken all the necessary precautions, but I accepted what she told me as fact and didn't insist on a paternity test." His voice became hard as his deep-seated anger crept into his words. "After we were married, I found out she lied to me. She made up the whole thing as a ruse to get me to marry her. I tried to make things work, but after we had been married for seven months, she ran off with the man she had been dating prior to me."

"I'm sorry." Her words came out as a whisper, as if she didn't know what else to say.

"That was ten years ago." He stiffened, uncomfortable with the direction the conversation had taken. He had let too many of his feelings show through. "It's ancient history and doesn't matter anymore."

Except, of course, it still mattered a great deal. So much so that he had allowed it to control his life in much the same manner as Darvi's past had controlled hers. Something they had in common, an emotional upheaval in each of their lives, in circumstances they shared. Circumstances that could end up tearing them apart.

He forced the sadness away and, along with it, his rising panic over his feeling of emotional attachment to Darvi. A realization that grew stronger and stronger with each passing day.

They snuggled under the down comforter as the rain continued to beat relentlessly against the roof. They shut out the world and existed solely for each other during the few remaining hours left to them before work would take priority over their personal lives for the duration of the project.

The storm increased in intensity. The howling wind rattled the windows, and the rain pounded on the roof and walls of her studio. The loud thunderclaps jarred them from a peaceful sleep. Rance switched on the bedside lamp. Jagged bolts of lightning streaked across the sky. The lights flickered then dimmed.

A strange uneasiness engulfed Darvi. As a child, thunderstorms had never been frightening. Her father had taught her to count the seconds between the flash of the lightning and the sound of the thunder to determine their distance from the storm and whether it was moving toward them or away. This little scientific experiment had made the entire mystique less scary and more of an intellectual adventure. But as an adult, specifically since the horrible night of her miscarriage, storms like this made her uneasy.

Her body stiffened as the lights went out completely, plunging the room into darkness. She reached out for the reassurance of his touch. "Rance…"

"I'm here. I'm right here. Everything's okay." He kissed her on the forehead and stroked her long hair as he rocked her in his arms. "This is very unusual, the thunder and lightning. Normally, it just rains and the wind blows."

A calm settled around her. Rance being there made everything okay. Her body relaxed. The flashes did not seem as bright, the noise not as loud.

The pendulum clock in the other room chimed three times as Rance seductively tickled his fingers up her inner thigh. The storm raged around them, but they shut it out as they sank into the sensual swirl of their passions.

****

By eight o'clock the next morning, power had been restored at Darvi's studio, the raging storm had settled into a moderate rain, and the wind had subsided. Rance stood at her opened front door, sipping hot coffee from a mug as he surveyed the scene. Trash cans littered the street. Small tree branches had been broken off, scattered on lawns, and across the pavement.

"You're letting in the cold air."

He quickly turned at the sound of her voice and gave her a warm, loving smile. "Hi." He held up his mug. "I took the liberty of making coffee. May I get you some?"

"Thanks, I already did." She lifted her coffee cup for his inspection, then directed her attention out the door. "How is it out there? Much damage?"

He closed the door and put his arm around her shoulders as they walked across the studio toward the kitchen. "All things considered, it's not bad. Runaway trash cans and some broken tree branches." His brow furrowed in concentration as he glanced out the kitchen window. "However, I should get home to check out my place before I stop by the construction site to see if Bill has any significant damage to report. If it's bad, I'm going to have to file an insurance claim, which will not set well with George."

"I hope everything's okay." She looked at her watch. "According to the schedule we set up yesterday afternoon, I'm already running an hour late. Looks like I'll have to work through lunch or stay overtime at my worktable tonight."

He grinned. "The first day and already the schedule is shot to hell." He took the last swallow of his coffee, set the mug in the kitchen sink, then reached for his jacket. "I'd better get going. I've lots of work to do, too." He pulled her into his arms and kissed her tenderly on the lips. "I'll call you this evening."

Darvi stood at the door and watched Rance dash to his car, dodging puddles on the way. She continued to watch until his car disappeared around the corner. She closed the door, then leaned against it, her eyes shut and a contented smile curling the corners of her mouth. *How did I ever get so lucky?*

The smile faded as a note of caution intruded into her moment of happy reflection. Could she be reading too much into the situation? Hoping for more than what really existed? Doing the same thing she had done with Jerry…*assuming* Rance felt the same way she did?

She didn't have time for the intrusive and bothersome thoughts. She shoved them away and turned her attention to the tight work schedule and everything she still had to do.

****

Rance braked the car to a screeching halt halfway up his driveway. Two of his trash barrels and a small branch from the tree next to the house blocked his way. He hit the remote control to open the garage door, but nothing happened. No electricity. Maybe Darvi had lucked out with getting power back right away, but he had not escaped the inconvenience brought by what could be a prolonged blackout.

He dashed to the side door of the garage and ducked in from the rain. Grabbing an old, hooded rain jacket from a hook, he slipped it on and manually unlocked and opened the garage door from the inside. He gave a brief thought to getting a new garage door with battery backup for just such occasions. He quickly dismissed the idea as irrelevant at the moment. After heaving a deep sigh of resignation, he ran back outside to clear the obstructions from his driveway.

By noon, his electricity had been restored. He called the construction site and Bill Jenkins assured him there wasn't any damage to speak of, no need for him to do a personal inspection. With everything apparently under control, he went to his workshop to check on the progress Bobby had made the previous day. Various types of wood were stacked in the corner. Bobby had spread out the pieces he had cut to the pattern specifications. They

---

Shawna Delacorte

were on the work bench for Rance's inspection. Rance would do the more difficult cutting with intricate twists and turns. Then, like a giant jigsaw puzzle, he would assemble the wood pieces into the desired pattern.

The falling rain hit the skylights and the sides of the barn, creating a steady background noise. The previous night's storm had cost him half a day. There used to be enough hours in the day to get everything done. Now, things had to be given priorities, time taken away from this and given to that. He furrowed his brow and slowly shook his head. An uncomfortable sensation ebbed and surged through his body, one he couldn't clearly identify. Once again, he wondered if he was getting in over his head with Darvi, taking on more than he could handle.

****

Amy packaged the purchases but held on to the bag as Darvi tried to take it. From the moment she entered Amy's shop, her friend's curiosity had been blatantly obvious, her desire to know about Darvi's relationship with Rance. As he had said, Sandy Cove was a small town, and the locals were aware of his car being at her studio all night.

Amy followed Darvi around making idle conversation with Rance's name figuring prominently in every other sentence. Darvi didn't know whether to be embarrassed, angry, admit everything, or pretend she didn't know what Amy meant.

Amy interrupted Darvi's musings. "And when I heard that Rance's car was in front of your place all night, I just didn't know what to think. Did he, uh, have some sort of car trouble?"

"Amy…" She looked at her friend and shook her head in resignation. She couldn't hold back her

132

amusement at being the center of local gossip. She let out a soft laugh. "No, Amy, as far as I know there wasn't anything wrong with Rance's car." She leaned across the counter and whispered in Amy's ear. "There's absolutely nothing wrong with Rance, either."

****

The digital clock in Rance's workshop read seven-fifteen. He hadn't stopped work for lunch. Dinner time had come and gone. Hunger pangs rumbled in his stomach, along with the occasional yawn reflecting his fatigue. He inspected his work area. All the smaller pieces for two of the doors had been cut and placed in order. He made a mental note of what had been accomplished, pleased to have the work back on schedule. He cleaned up the sawdust and wood shavings, then turned out the lights in his workshop.

After he finished eating, he almost climbed into his truck and drove to Darvi's studio. He wanted to see her, hear the sound of her voice, touch her, hold her. She filled his every thought. Instead, he stifled a yawn, then reached for the phone and dialed her number. He disconnected the call before the phone rang. No, he wouldn't put himself in the position of pursuing her any more than he already had. He needed to find a balance, to get control of the rapidly escalating situation.

The following weeks passed quickly. Darvi and Rance stuck to their schedules during the day, both working at a feverish pace to finish as soon as possible. Rance had completed all the custom doors. He spent most of his time at the construction site, overseeing the final stages of the renovations. The doors would be hung in place last, after all the other work had been completed. In fact, they were actually a week ahead of schedule, only one week away from completion. George made periodic checks on the progress, each time more pleased with what he saw than he had been with his previous inspection.

The stained-glass windows were installed in each of the guest rooms, but Darvi still had to finish the lobby. Their large size dictated they be done in sections. The project had gone flawlessly in spite of the series of storms that had swept in from the Pacific Ocean, causing sporadic power outages and flooded roads.

Despite Rance's intention to slow down his growing involvement with Darvi, the two of them spent nights and weekends together, along with any other time they could spare. They took long walks on the beach, wrapped in warm coats to ward off the cold ocean wind. They ate dinner on the floor of his living room in front of the fireplace, warmed by the roaring flames.

On one unusually nice Sunday, they went horseback riding. They hiked through the woods in the surrounding mountains. And the previous weekend he had taken her to Portland to meet his family. They had stayed with his sister. Rance's family adored her just as much as she adored them.

The sight of the two of them together had become a common occurrence in Sandy Cove. They were no longer an interesting item for the local gossips. No one cared anymore whose car remained parked at whose place all night long. The thought of combining their work studios and possibly their living arrangements had popped into Rance's mind from time to time, but he had shoved the prospect aside.

To act on that possibility would definitely signal a firm pledge for the future, a step he still wasn't ready to take. Even though he had reluctantly accepted the truth, the fact that he was falling in love with Darvi—had already fallen in love with her—taking that final step to a total commitment frightened him. Things were good between them just as they were without the complication of dwelling on plans for the future.

****

Darvi lay snuggled in Rance's arms beneath the flowered canopy of her bed. She kissed the warm skin of his hard chest before resting her head against his shoulder.

He gently stroked her hair and ran his fingertips across her creamy skin. "The inn will be finished in another ten days. George has planned an invitation-only open house a week from this Saturday."

She wrapped her arm around his torso, listened to his strong heartbeat, and felt his breathing. "I know. We'll be finished ahead of schedule. I can't believe everything that's happened in the last couple of months." A flush of embarrassment heated her cheeks at the implications of what she had just said. "I mean, all the work that's been accomplished at the inn."

He touched his lips to her forehead, and she snuggled closer to him. "I've had a call from some builders in Portland. George showed them photographs of the doors I did for the inn. They want me to come up and meet with them about doing some custom woodwork in a hotel they're building. I need to leave next Tuesday. I'll be gone for three or four days, but I'll be back in time for the open house."

She looked up at him, her gaze locking with his. "I'll miss you."

"I'll be staying with my sister if you need to get in

touch with me." The thought of even three or four days away from her upset him. He remained silent, afraid to speak until he had his emotions firmly under control. "Will you be finished with the lobby windows by next Tuesday? You could come with me."

"No, unfortunately I won't be. I ran out of yellow stain. Amy had to do a special order, and it won't be in until that Monday. Once I get my hands on it, I'll have about three day's work to do before I'm finished."

What Darvi did not tell Rance was that she had not been feeling well lately. She felt tired, rundown, and occasionally nauseous in the morning. During his absence, she would make an appointment with a doctor. She wanted to feel her best for the open house. She probably had some kind of a flu bug, nothing more. At least she wanted to believe it.

Yet in the back of her mind lurked a thought so frightening she refused to give it any credence.

Chapter Nine

Darvi sat on the edge of her bed looking at the slip of paper Amy had given her with the name and phone number of her doctor in Summitville. A cold fear shivered up her spine as she reached for the phone and dialed the number.

The receptionist said there had been a cancellation. The doctor could see her on Thursday morning at ten o'clock. Since she was a new patient, she would have an additional half hour with the doctor to go over her medical history. Darvi provided the name of her physician in Laguna Beach so her files could be sent prior to her appointment.

She spent the rest of Tuesday and all of Wednesday finishing the lobby windows so the last remaining sections could be put in place first thing Thursday morning. The carpeting had already been installed. Most of the furniture had been delivered, and the interior decorator had most of the accents in place. There remained only the final decorating touches, then Saturday evening would be the open house party before the grand opening.

Thursday morning, Darvi drove the fifteen miles to Summitville. Her nerves played havoc with her senses as she waited to see the doctor. The nurse instructed her to fill out what seemed like mountains of forms. After taking her height, weight, and blood pressure, the nurse showed her into an office to wait for the doctor.

"You're Darvi Stanton?"

She turned at the sound of the male voice and saw a pleasant-looking man in his early fifties. She answered, her voice sounding not as firm as she would have liked. "Yes."

He shook her hand and smiled. "I'm Dr. Hartner." He seated himself behind the desk and placed the file he'd brought with him next to the forms Darvi had filled out. He quickly glanced over the forms. "I see you're a friend of Amy Sutter's. How is Amy these days?"

Amy had told her she saw Dr. Hartner a week ago. The doctor was obviously making small talk to put her at ease. "She's fine. The art supply store is busy and doing well."

"That's good. I've known Amy and Frank for several years. They're good people." He opened the file he had brought with him and scanned the entries, then set it aside and looked at Darvi. "Now, what brings you here today?"

She hesitated before speaking, trying to decide precisely what to say. "I'm not exactly sure why I'm here. I've been feeling a little tired lately, run down, and sometimes, my stomach is a bit queasy. I've been working pretty hard of late. I think it's probably just a touch of the flu. I have an important function this weekend and don't want to be sick. I thought maybe you could give me a shot of something…a vitamin shot."

"I see." The doctor flipped through her file again. "When was the last time you saw a doctor?"

She hesitated. "It was the follow-up to my miscarriage, about two years ago."

"Well, let's get a little more information here. Have

you had any problems since the miscarriage?"

"None that I can think of."

"When was your last menstrual period?"

Darvi furrowed her brow in thought. "I guess about eight or so weeks ago…maybe longer." She considered the response she had given the doctor. She became less confident with each ensuing word. "It was about the same time I moved to Oregon. I guess that would be closer to ten or twelve weeks ago."

The doctor put down his pen and gazed at her, a note of caution in his voice. "Eight weeks…maybe closer to ten or even twelve weeks?"

She quickly interjected, "Oh, that's sort of normal for me. I've always been somewhat irregular, and since the miscarriage, seven weeks or so between periods has been fairly common." Her brow furrowed again. "Of course, it has been longer than that…"

Dr. Hartner looked through the file again. "I don't see any prescribed form of birth control here. Are you sexually active at this time or have you been since moving to Oregon?"

Heat rose on her cheeks as she lowered her eyes. "Yes." Her gaze shot back to the doctor's face as she realized the implications of his words. "But I couldn't be pregnant. Following the accident and miscarriage, the doctor said I wasn't able to have any more children."

Dr. Hartner again scanned the file, a hint of a frown creasing his forehead. "I don't see any mention of that. Are you sure that's what he said? That must have been a highly emotional and stressful time for you. Perhaps you misunderstood him. There is a notation here that you were cautioned about not becoming pregnant again too soon after the miscarriage."

"But, Dr. Hartner, I can't be pregnant." Panic welled inside her as her deepest fear slammed into her.

"Oh, I'm afraid you can and very well might be. The lab will tell us for sure."

Tears welled in Darvi's eyes as she fought to maintain her control. "But you don't understand. I told Rance birth control wasn't necessary, that I couldn't have any children. How can I go back to him now and tell him it was all a mistake? Nothing more than just one of those little *misunderstandings*?"

"You say *go back to him*. Is the relationship no longer valid? Are you no longer seeing this man?"

"I didn't mean it that way. We're still seeing each other. It's just that…" She fought to keep control of her emotions. "How can I do this to him?"

The doctor reached over, smiled comfortingly, and patted her hand. "Let's not get ourselves upset when we don't know for sure that there's any reason to be upset. Do you love this man?"

"Yes, very much."

"And does he love you?"

She hesitated a moment. "I…I don't know."

She had never asked herself that question, and Rance had never really said anything definite about his feelings. Somewhere in the back of her mind, she had been afraid of what the answer might be.

"There shouldn't be anything the two of you can't work out if you love each other. Let's find out if you have the flu or something a little more tangible."

After an exam and tests, Darvi returned to Sandy Cove. Her stomach hadn't stopped churning from the moment she realized she could possibly be pregnant. She tried to eat something for dinner, but finally gave up. She paced up and down her bedroom, nervously waiting for Rance's call. He had phoned her every night about this time.

When he called her Wednesday night, he told her he wouldn't be home until late Friday night. He had meetings all day and a dinner meeting that evening. Normally, he would have stayed over Friday night and driven home Saturday morning, but he wanted to be back to help with the arrangements for the open house party Saturday night.

She had decided not to tell him about the doctor and the probable truth of her pregnancy until the lab confirmed it. No reason for both of them to be upset. The lab results would be available to her the next day, on Friday. When he arrived Friday night, she would know one way or the other. His words about his ex-wife's faked pregnancy played over and over in her mind, and each time, she heard the anger, bitterness, and resentment in his voice when he had told her about it. And each time, she heard it in her head even louder than the time before.

Friday felt like pure torture. Time seemed to move at a snail's pace. Even though she didn't want to hear the test results, she had to set her fears aside and face the probable truth. She glanced at the phone for the hundredth time, then forced her attention back to work.

The dreaded call finally arrived. She gulped in a steadying breath, then reached for the phone. She listened to the test results. "Yes…thank you for calling."

Darvi's trembling hand still rested on the phone as she sat on the edge of the bed, her insides twisted into tight knots. Fear ricocheted through her body. Tears welled in her eyes. The lab results revealed the last thing she wanted to hear, the reality she feared the most. She was pregnant. The probable date of conception was the first time she and Rance had made love. Even if they had taken precautions after that, it would have been too late.

She tried to remain calm, to deal with the situation logically. The first thing she needed to do was tell Rance. He would be home that night. She would tell him as soon as he arrived. Again, his angry words about being tricked into marriage by a woman who falsely claimed to be pregnant with his child filled her head. Hard spasms of fear rocked her body. A sick sensation churned in her stomach. Was it pregnancy or anxiety? She wasn't sure.

Darvi nervously paced up and down the floor as she glanced at the clock for what seemed like the hundredth time. Almost midnight. Where could he be? She had expected him home before now, even with the stormy weather.

This time, the waiting felt worse than when she had told Jerry about being pregnant. At that time, she had visualized how wonderful everything would be, how happy Jerry would be at the news. She had visualized their future together as a family, how it would be so perfect. But this time was different. She loved Rance so much. If he rejected the baby—rejected her—she didn't know what she would do.

Her brow furrowed as an uncomfortable thought struck her. The situation now with Rance and the circumstances then with Jerry weren't really that different after all. She didn't think there was any danger of pregnancy then, just as she hadn't believed she could get pregnant now. Rance was out of town on business and didn't know about her doctor's appointment, just as Jerry had been out of town and had not known she went to the doctor.

She looked out the window. A cold shiver went through her as she wondered what other similarities there would be. She heard the patter of the raindrops on the roof and windows of her studio. The last loose end. It had been raining that night, too.

The storm came from the north. Rance had probably been driving in rain all the way from Portland. He would be exhausted when he arrived. Perhaps it would be better if she told him about the baby in the morning after he had gotten some sleep. She wrinkled her brow into a frown. Tomorrow was the open house. They would both be involved with the preparations, and tomorrow evening, they would be greeting and mingling with the guests. There wouldn't be enough time to deal with such an important situation as her pregnancy, not enough time to talk about it. Perhaps after the party would be better.

Her nerves jittered through her body, then knotted into a hard lump in the pit of her stomach. She tasted the fear welling inside her and rising up her throat. Peering out the front door, she tried to stare through the darkness and the rain, tried to force him to materialize from out of the night.

****

Rance strained to see through the windshield of his car, but the pounding rain made it almost impossible. Any sane, normal person would have stopped driving and found a place to stay for the night or at least pulled off the road until the rain let up, but not him. He had to get home, to get back to Darvi. He had missed her so much it was almost unbearably painful. He had not realized exactly how much he loved her until he had been separated from her for the last four days. He was also worried.

For some reason—he couldn't put his finger on exactly what—he had been uneasy about leaving her. Something was wrong. He didn't know what, and she gave him no clue. He heard the stress in her voice the last time they talked on the phone. He needed to be home with her instead of out on some rain-swept highway battling the elements of nature.

He had pulled into a roadside rest and tried to call her but couldn't get a signal for his cell phone. Most likely due to the storm. Another fifty miles and he would have Darvi in his arms.

Myriad thoughts danced through his mind, the primary theme being about the two of them spending the rest of their lives together. A note of sadness picked at his senses. When she told him she couldn't have any more children, the only thing it had meant to him at the time was that he didn't need to be concerned with birth control. But now, thoughts of a family had entered his mind, thoughts he had never before seriously entertained. And those thoughts confused him. He didn't know what to make of them.

Rance peered through the windshield at the road ahead. His body ached with exhaustion as he blinked several times to ward off the sleep causing his eyelids to grow heavy. A soft smile curled the corners of his mouth. He had made his decision. He would tell Darvi how much he loved her right after the open house. A warm glow suffused him as he continued to drive toward his waiting happiness.

****

The insistent buzzing of the doorbell finally penetrated Darvi's sleep-clogged mind. She threw back the cover and rose from the couch where she had fallen asleep. She glanced at the clock. A little after two in the morning. A gust of cold, wet air rushed in as she opened the door.

Rance quickly stepped inside, closing the door behind him.

He dropped his suitcase on the floor, shed his wet rain jacket, and swept her into his arms in one smooth motion. His warm breath tickled across her cheek as his hands caressed her shoulders and back.

"The rain was rotten, traffic slow, terrible roads, and I couldn't get a signal to call you. I didn't think I was ever going to get here." His mouth dropped to hers, his kiss conveying all the longing and love he felt.

It all happened so fast. One minute, they stood by the front door, locked in each other's embrace, and the next minute, they were in the bedroom with Rance's clothes draped across a chair and his tall frame stretched out on her bed. Before she even had a chance to slide under the blankets next to him, she heard the slow, even rhythm of his breathing. He had fallen asleep.

Her eyes lovingly surveyed his tired, drawn face. He had pushed himself to the limit to be with her, rather than stay in Portland one more night. She wouldn't wake him. He needed the rest. She decided not to wait until after the open house. She would tell him about the baby in the morning. She slipped into bed, nestled next to him, and drifted off as she pressed her body against his warm skin.

****

Rance sat bolt upright, the chiming clock jarring him into wakefulness. He had shut down the second his head hit the pillow, both mind and body. He had fought to stay awake the last twenty miles of the drive. The only thing that had kept him going was the knowledge that he would soon be with Darvi, holding her, caressing her.

Loving her.

Rance grabbed his watch from the nightstand and focused on the time. Noon? It couldn't be. He climbed out of bed and cautiously peeked through the opened door, not wanting to barge naked into her studio without first making sure no one else was there.

The studio was as quiet and empty as her bedroom. He went to the bathroom where he found a note taped to the mirror. He quickly scanned the familiar handwriting.

George needed me at the inn to help with the preparations for the open house tonight. I didn't have the heart to wake you. He would like you there, too, as soon as you're up and about.

He felt a warm glow inside as he smiled and removed the note from the mirror. He softly whispered the words he couldn't keep inside. "I love you more than I thought possible to love anyone."

Rance closed his eyes and visualized her face. He had made the commitment in his mind, a commitment to Darvi and to their future together. He didn't like the current arrangement of his sleeping at her place, her sleeping at his place, their sleeping apart. He wanted them to have one home together, to be a family.

He remembered the pain in her eyes when she told him she couldn't have any more children. He wanted to have kids, for his and Darvi's love to produce another life. But, if it was not to be, that was okay, too. As long as they were together, nothing else mattered. He quickly dressed, grabbed his suitcase, and headed home. He needed to shower and change clothes.

Rance finally showed up at the inn about one-thirty

just as everyone was returning from lunch. He immediately spotted Darvi. A warm smile curled his mouth as he moved to her side, put his arm around her shoulders, and kissed her cheek.

"Good morning." He glanced at his watch. "Make that good afternoon. I'm sorry I conked out on you like that. I guess I was more exhausted than I realized. You should have yelled at me when you got up this morning."

She slipped her arm around his waist as they walked from the parking lot toward the inn. "You were tired—you needed the sleep. What time did you finally get up? George phoned me at nine o'clock, and the ringing phone didn't seem to put a dent in your reality."

"I really was out of it. Your noisy clock got me up. By the time it arrived at the twelfth chime, I was awake."

"You lolled around in bed until noon?"

He flashed a sexy grin as he pulled her around the corner of the building. "Yeah, and it wasn't easy, either. I was alone. I *loll* better when I have someone with me."

"Oh?" Her eyes sparkled. "Anyone in particular?"

"How many choices do I get?" he teased her, his heart overflowing with love.

"You'd better not need more than one." Darvi reached her arms around his neck as he enfolded her in his embrace. She looked lovingly into his eyes. "I missed you. I'm glad you're back." Then the loving look changed to one of anxiety. "Rance, there's something…"

She rested her head against his shoulder as if unable to continue with what she had tried to say.

A tremor started deep inside Rance and moved outward. He had been correct. Something was wrong. Trepidation churned inside him as he held her close and stroked her hair. "Darvi? What's the matter?"

She pulled away as she gave him a smile. "We'd better get inside before they send a search party for us."

He did not smile. Instead, he clenched his jaw in determination. "You can't put me off that easily. Something's wrong. Tell me what it is."

The smile faded from her lips, and her eyes became frightened. She quickly glanced back toward the parking lot. Her hands went to his chest as she pushed herself back from his arms. "Rance, we're attracting an audience. We really ought to get inside with the others." Her voice softened to a whisper, almost pleading. "Please, can we go inside?"

Her words were said with almost the same intonation as when she had tried to put off telling him about her past. If there was something new going on that had anywhere near the impact on her as that had, he wanted to know about it now.

"We're going to talk about this—whatever *this* is—before the day is through." He uttered the words with an unintended brusqueness, but the result ended up the same as if he had been able to control his tone. He left no room for objection or compromise.

"Yes, we have to talk but not right now and certainly not here." She turned and walked toward the front door of the inn leaving Rance standing by the wall, stunned at her response, and with his insides tied in knots.

****

George was a bundle of nervous energy as he hurried from one room to the next. It was already five o'clock. The invitations stated cocktails and hors d'oeuvres at six-thirty with live music and dancing. The list of invitees included local city officials and everyone connected with the renovations no matter how small the connection, the inn's newly hired manager, new chef, travel agents, travel magazine writers, and photographers.

Newspaper and television media representatives from California, Oregon, Washington, Arizona, and Nevada had been invited—even some influential bloggers and others with internet and social media presence connected to the travel industry. If people with power to entice and recommend were suitably impressed, the success of the inn would be assured.

Caterers and musicians were on the scene setting up their equipment and preparing for the evening. Darvi had excused herself at four o'clock to go home, take a bath, and dress. Rance wanted to go with her, but she put him off by telling him she wouldn't be that long. She assured him they would have time together following the open house.

Rance stood at the inn's front door and watched her walk to her car as he tried to fight his mounting anxiety.

"Rance? Are you okay?"

Amy's voice intruded on his thoughts. "What? Oh, yeah, I'm fine. Why do you ask?"

"You looked like you were on Mars or somewhere equally far away." She cautiously continued. "Is it Darvi? Is she okay?"

He eyed her suspiciously. "Why wouldn't she be okay?"

Amy obviously realized she had said something wrong and quickly tried to recover. "Oh, no reason. She had mentioned being a little rundown, then when she went to see the doctor—"

"Darvi went to see a doctor while I was out of town?" Rance couldn't stop his eyes from widening in shock, an expression that stopped Amy in midsentence.

She made an obvious attempt to sound casual. "Oh, you know. It's probably just one of those flu things that's always going around. I'm sure it's nothing to worry about. Otherwise she would have said something." She glanced across the room. "Frank looks lost. I think he needs me." She gave Rance a tentative smile and hurried off.

Rance's heart pounded. He had difficulty getting his mind wrapped around what Amy had said. *Darvi went to the doctor? Why didn't she tell me?*

The fog began to clear from his head to be immediately replaced by panic, full-on panic almost bordering on an all-out anxiety attack.

He wheeled around and walked, almost ran, to the front door of the inn and headed out to the parking lot. He needed to get to Darvi, find out what was wrong, determine if she was all right. *If? IF? Of course she's all right...she has to be all right.*

He pushed past several people, not even acknowledging them. He ignored George's attempt to speak to him as he ran across the parking lot to his car. But then he sat with his car engine running and the transmission in gear. He slowly reached over and turned off the ignition.

She said we'd have time to ourselves following the open house. I'll give her through tonight to tell me about the doctor. He slowly bent forward until his forehead rested against the steering wheel, his hands gripping it tightly, his eyes shut. He shuddered as the full emotional impact raced through him. *She has to be okay—she just has to be okay.*

He started his car again and drove home to change

clothes for the evening's festivities even though he didn't feel very festive. When he returned to the inn, he spotted Darvi the moment he entered the lobby. His heart instantly swelled with the love he felt for her. A love deeper and more intense than he ever believed possible.

He crossed the room to Darvi and placed his arm around her shoulders, protectively drawing her to his side. He leaned his mouth to her ear. "You look beautiful. The other women here might as well go home right now because no one will notice them after everyone gets a look at you." He fixed her with a mischievous grin. "In fact, you look absolutely delicious." He held on to her for a long moment, filled with the warmth and love he felt for her. "Run away with me right now. No one will even miss us."

Chapter Ten

The love Rance felt for Darvi continued to do battle with his anxiety over what secret she was keeping from him, a secret that involved a trip to the doctor. He tried to push his anxiety aside, to focus on the happy feelings.

"Run away with me," he repeated his suggestion. "We can find a private hideaway for just the two of us. The days will be warm and clear, the air filled with the fragrance of a thousand flowers. We'll take long walks in the woods and along the beach. At night, we'll count the stars and make love in the soft glow of the moon. It will be just the two of us. We'll have no cares and no worries."

Darvi rested her head against his shoulder and sighed as she laced her fingers through his. "You're very persuasive. I see and feel everything you're saying, and it sounds wonderful."

He took a deep, steadying breath, then swallowed to clear his dry throat. The time was now. He would tell her of his love. He continued, tentatively and cautiously. "It is possible, you know. We can do just that. Maybe we can't stay there forever, but—"

"Hey, you two." The abrupt intrusion came from Bill Jenkins. "Are you going to stand here huddled in the corner, playing kissy-face forever? Guests are arriving. It's time to circulate and be charming, sell the hell out of this place."

Rance looked up and saw that guests really were arriving. Some of them he recognized as locals, but others were from out of town. He looked into Darvi's eyes. "Apparently we're *on*." He brushed his lips quickly against hers. "We'll pursue this conversation later."

He took her hand and led her to the front door where George was busy greeting the arrivals.

The evening turned out to be a huge success with everyone having a wonderful time. The people who needed to be impressed seemed to be just that. What was supposed to have lasted until nine o'clock continued until well after one in the morning. The caterers brought in more food and drink. The musicians agreed to stay and play as long as people wanted to dance.

Rance watched Darvi closely. She seemed to be having fun. He did not notice any tension or stress, did not see any anxiety or apprehension. On the surface, it appeared whatever had been bothering her had vanished.

They danced to every slow song. He held her closely, reveling in the silkiness of her skin and the enticing scent of her perfume. But one thought kept repeating itself over and over. Why had she gone to the doctor, and why didn't she tell him?

The hour had reached well after midnight when he spotted Darvi in a far corner huddled with a stranger. They seemed totally absorbed in their conversation. Rance made his way across the room toward them.

Darvi smiled at him as he approached. "Rance Coulter, this is Barney Daniels." She turned her attention to Barney as the two men shook hands. "Rance is the contractor on this job. He also made all the custom designed wooden doors for the rooms."

She directed her next comments to Rance.

"Barney's a contractor, too. He came with his wife this evening. She's a travel agent. Barney and I were discussing a house he's remodeling in Summitville. The owners have expressed an interest in some stained-glass window insets for the double doors at the entrance. I'm going to drive over on Monday and take a look at what they have in mind and see if I can come up with something they like."

Darvi turned her attention to Barney as she held up his business card. "I'll stop by your office about ten o'clock Monday morning if that's okay."

Barney extended his hand to Darvi. "I look forward to it." He turned to Rance and shook his hand. "Rance, it's a pleasure." He glanced toward the inn's front door. "Now, I'd better catch up with my wife before she runs off and abandons me."

They watched as Barney walked across the lobby, then Darvi turned excitedly to Rance. "He really liked my work. He says he has several projects in the planning stage and might be able to use my talents often." She smiled. "Isn't that thrilling? I was a little worried when I moved up here, wasn't sure exactly how much work I'd be able to generate, how far away from Sandy Cove I'd be able to reach out for clients."

Rance put his arm around her shoulders and gave a squeeze as he smiled at her. "That's great." A sudden thought hit him. "Hey, why don't I go with you on Monday? I don't have anything to do that can't wait until Tuesday. We could have lunch in Summitville before driving home. I know a charming little Italian restaurant on a bluff overlooking the ocean."

"Actually, I have some personal errands to run. It would just be boring for you." She offered him a hesitant but reassuring smile. "I promise to be back by early afternoon." She had not offered him the complete truth. She had a personal errand all right—an appointment with Dr. Hartner.

Rance furrowed his brow. *She blatantly put me off with a flimsy excuse. She doesn't want me to go to Summitville with her. Why?* He tightened his hold on her. A shiver of fear darted through him. "Sure, that will be okay. I do have some preliminary designs to do for the Portland project."

Darvi's face lit up. "Oh! Did you get the job?"

"Nothing's official until there's a signed contract, but we shook hands on the deal."

She threw her arms around his neck as she beamed her happiness. "I'm so thrilled about your news."

He felt the tension in her body as he spoke softly in her ear. "Let's go home. I have something I want to say to you, and this isn't the place."

She put her hand against his cheek. "I'm very tired. It's been an incredibly busy day."

His words circulated through her mind, words about the two of them running away. Only it's no longer just the two of them. Then she flashed on his bitterness and anger about his ex-wife's claim of pregnancy. Perhaps it would be better to wait and tell him after her doctor appointment on Monday, after she was able to confirm the pregnancy with her doctor in person rather than merely accepting the result from a phone call.

She took a steadying breath in an attempt to settle her rattled nerves. "Could whatever it is keep for a while?"

He peered into the emerald depths of her eyes and saw her fear. An intense battle raged within him. One side demanded to know what had her so frightened while the other side wanted to give her the room she seemed to be desperately seeking. He rested his cheek against the top of her head and let out a sigh. "I don't know what this is about, but you apparently want some space and some time."

He leaned back and looked into her very soul. "I'll give you the space, but I can't give you much more time." He pulled her to him again. "I'll give you until Monday evening. If you haven't told me what this is about by then, I'm going to pester you nonstop until you confess everything. I won't give you a moment's rest until I know for sure that everything is all right."

Her soft voice—her *frightened* voice—conveyed barely audible words. "Fair enough."

The next morning, storm clouds threatened on the horizon. Rance and Darvi made their way across the lobby of the inn to the cozy setting by the fireplace where Amy, Frank, and George waited for them. It was smiles all around as they greeted everyone.

George held up his coffee cup. "I'd like to propose a toast. To all of you and everyone else who worked so hard to make last night a great success. Words alone can't express how much I appreciate your efforts."

He put his cup down on the end table next to his chair. "I've been getting feedback all morning and every bit of it very positive. There will be a two-page spread in the travel section of next Sunday's Portland newspaper." They all beamed their pleasure at the news. "And two weeks from today the Sunday magazine supplement of the Seattle paper will carry an article with color photos. The San Francisco paper will be doing the same thing. And even in Canada…I heard that the Vancouver Sun might run an article about the inn.

"And you two—" George looked at Rance and Darvi. "—I can't begin to tell you how many words of praise I heard about your work. Everyone loved it. The stained-glass windows are beautiful." He addressed his next comments to Rance. "This is the smoothest construction job I've ever been involved with. You had a top-notch crew. Everything was professional and first-class. I'm glad you talked me into the custom-designed doors. They added just that special touch to the hallways."

"Thanks, George. That's nice of you to say." Rance smiled at him, then looked at Darvi and gave her hand a squeeze. "Thanks needs to go to Bill Jenkins, too. He's a top-rate construction foreman and really kept the crew on schedule so we could stay on budget, which allowed me the time to make the custom doors."

Everyone was in high spirits as they talked about the previous night's open house. Darvi excused herself a couple of times to go to the restroom. The second time, Amy quietly excused herself and followed.

As soon as they were alone in the restroom, Amy immediately turned to Darvi. "Does he know yet? Have you told Rance?"

Darvi feigned ignorance at her question. "Does Rance know what? What are you talking about, Amy?"

Amy looked at her for a long moment. "I'm talking about you being pregnant."

Darvi's eyes opened wide in shock. "But how—"

Amy put her arm reassuringly around Darvi's shoulders. "It's so obvious. You know, Rance is worried sick about you. Whenever he thinks no one is watching, his entire face shows his concern. Don't you think it's time you told him?"

"Oh, Amy, I don't know what to do." She sank into a chair as tears welled in her eyes. "It's more than just my being pregnant. All I keep thinking about is the situation with his ex-wife."

The confusion covered Amy's face. "His ex-wife? Rance has been divorced for about ten years. What would his ex-wife have to do with this?"

"Didn't you know? She tricked him into marriage by telling him she was pregnant. You can't imagine the anger and bitterness in his voice when he told me about it, even after all these years. What if he thinks I'm doing the same thing?"

"I can't believe Rance would think that of you. You have to tell him before any more time goes by."

"Of course, I have to tell him. I just don't know how. I keep putting it off while I try to figure out the best way to do it, the right words to say."

After about fifteen minutes, the two women returned to the lobby. As they sat down, Frank glanced at his watch, then at Rance. "Have you ever noticed that one woman in a bathroom takes twice as much time as any man, and *two* women in a bathroom…"

Amy glared at him, then broke out in a laugh. "This, coming from a man who takes half an hour just to decide what temperature he wants the shower."

Everyone's spirits seemed light, but Rance watched Darvi carefully, looking for any signs that would tell him what was going on. He was positive she and Amy had been talking about it, whatever *it* was. After all, Amy knew she had been to the doctor. What could she confide to Amy but couldn't tell him? Somewhere in the back of his mind a frightening thought tried to force its way into his consciousness, a fear that she might be sick, that her life might be in danger, but he refused to allow it. He could not consider that possibility.

It was mid afternoon before they left the inn. The wind had picked up with storm clouds closing in. They were in for another storm before the day was out.

Darvi and Rance hurried to his car, the cold wind whipping around them. He held her hand as he drove to her place in silence. He was torn between taking her home and leaving her alone, as she had requested, or demanding she immediately tell him what was bothering her.

He stood inside Darvi's front door, preparing to leave. "Now remember, you have only until tomorrow evening to tell me what's going on here."

He looked at the blackening sky and threatening storm clouds. "It appears that we're in for quite a downpour. Are you sure you want to be alone? I could stay. I promise I'll be as quiet as a mouse."

She placed her hand lovingly against his cheek as she brushed his lips with a kiss. "It isn't whether or not you're making noise. Your mere presence is totally distracting to me." She looked into his eyes, silently pleading for just a little more understanding, just a little more blind faith. "I can't think when you're around me."

He scowled. "I don't like it, Darvi. I don't like knowing something is wrong and you're not telling me what it is." He touched his finger to the tip of her nose. "Remember—tomorrow evening and not one minute longer."

His manner softened as he wrapped her in his arms. His mouth captured hers, the kiss lasting only a moment. "I'm just a phone call away if you need me."

He forced a smile, not at all as confident as the image he projected. He held her gaze for a few seconds, then he opened the door and left.

Darvi shivered when the strong gust of cold, damp air hit her before she could close the door. She walked slowly into her bedroom, her mind racing in a thousand directions at once as she pondered her dilemma.

How do I tell him he's going to be a father? That I'm carrying his child? What will he think? How will he react?

Once again, the thought popped into her mind. He had talked about them running away to some enchanted place…just the two of them. How would he feel when she told him there would be *three* of them? The knots in her stomach grew tighter and tighter with each passing minute.

Does he really love me? Is it possible for him to love me as much as I love him? Will he want me after he finds out I'm pregnant? I have to tell him. Amy's right, I can't wait much longer.

So many questions and no answers. She went to bed, intending to read for a while.

The storm hit about eleven o'clock that night. The rain pounded against the windows and on the roof. Darvi lay in bed, listening to the howling wind as it whipped around the studio and through the trees. She huddled under the covers, feeling so very alone in the large bed. She had become accustomed to Rance's body next to hers as she slept whether in her bed or his bed, his warmth radiating to her, his strength being hers.

After much agonizing, she finally made her decision about telling him. Dr. Hartner's office had already confirmed her pregnancy. She had no reason to wait until after she had seen him again. She would just say it straight out and hope he accepted it without being upset or angry. Even if the lab had made an error and she wasn't really pregnant, he still had to be told that they needed to take precautions starting immediately.

The stress weighed heavily on her from all directions, welling inside her until there wasn't any more room. She never should have let Rance go home. She wanted the comfort of his arms. He needed to know about the pregnancy…and that she loved him. It was the type of thing that had to be done in person rather than an impersonal phone call. She dressed quickly then darted through the rain to her car.

****

The insistent buzzing of the doorbell finally shook Rance out of his sleep. He pulled on a pair of sweatpants, went to the door, and angrily yanked it open. The cold air rushed in, hitting his face, bare chest, and feet.

"Darvi!" He reached out and pulled her inside, quickly closing the door behind her.

"We have to talk. It can't wait until tomorrow night."

Something about her expression and the stress in her voice put him on alert. "Of course, but why didn't you call? I would have driven to your place. You shouldn't be out in this weather. The roads are far too dangerous."

"I…I've put this off too long as it is, trying to find the proper words and the right time. It can't wait any longer."

Hard bands tightened across his chest as apprehension seeped into his consciousness. His defense mechanism kicked in, the instinct to protect himself, to hide the vulnerability rising inside him. A moment of panic grabbed his reality, seemingly taking control of his thoughts and actions. Rather than pulling her securely into his embrace and showing his care and concern, he stepped back and folded his arms across his chest. "So, what seems to be your problem?"

Rance's abrupt change in attitude caught Darvi by surprise. He seemed suddenly distant, literally backing away from her. His voice had turned cold. Did he suspect the truth? Were her fears and confusion dictating her thoughts? Or was he already blaming her? Then another thought hit her, a frightening one. Did he believe she was trying to manipulate him just as his ex-wife had?

She swallowed hard, trying to ease the lump in her throat. Could she be over analyzing the situation? Jumping to conclusions without any facts? Or was she grasping at straws?

She searched his face for some clue to his feelings, his mood or, more accurately, his sudden change in mood. She saw what looked like thousands of thoughts and emotions darting through his eyes, all of them enveloped in caution and uncertainty. The tremors started small then quickly spread through her body as her worst fear enveloped her.

"Well, I went to the doctor on Thursday and…uh…he did some tests and…" Her gaze darted nervously around the room, landing briefly on some object, then moving quickly to another. Her hands twisted in the bottom of her sweatshirt. Her mouth went dry, and her stomach clenched in knots.

"And what?"

A hard edge clung to his voice. An intensity covered his face, an expression that frightened her, one far removed from caring and understanding. A sick churning worked its way up from the pit of her stomach. Her words caught in her throat and refused to leave.

His voice grew louder—and angry. "And what, Darvi? What the hell's going on here? You went to the doctor, and he did some tests. Then what? Come on, out with it!"

She clamped her eyes shut. Pain throbbed at her temples. "I'm pregnant. I'm about two months along."

The silence hung heavily in the air. Several long moments ticked off before he responded to what she had said. Each moment felt to her like an hour. An agonizing hour.

"What do you mean you're pregnant? What the hell are you talking about? You assured me you couldn't have any children. Was that a lie? Some kind of a con?"

His voice sounded remote, disconnected, unbelieving. And definitely accusatory. She didn't know what his reaction would be, but this was far removed from what she had anticipated. The knot in her stomach pulled tighter to the point where it had become physically uncomfortable. A sick sensation rose in her throat.

She had hoped he would be happy, that they would be a family. She thought she had learned from her past mistakes. She truly believed Rance was so different from Jerry. Obviously, she had seriously misjudged things. She hadn't made a plan for handling the situation if it went wrong. And this couldn't have gone more wrong.

All the defensiveness she hid behind for two years suddenly sprang to the forefront, once again providing that protective wall that, in the past, had shielded her from the emotional pain and turmoil. She made a desperate attempt at shoving away the despair rapidly enveloping her. "I'm talking about me being pregnant with your child. The doctor confirmed it. I didn't lie to you. I truly believed I couldn't conceive children. Her voice was caustic, but she could not hide the hurt running rampant inside her.

All the bitterness and anger associated with the circumstances of his short-lived marriage flooded into Rance's mind. He didn't seem to have any control over his words or actions. He wasn't talking to Darvi. In his mind, he was involved in a showdown with Joan over her lies and manipulation. "What the hell's going on here? What are you trying to pull? That ploy worked once before, so you thought it would work again? Is that your game?

Darvi felt physically ill, her mouth and throat as dry as the Sahara Desert. Her mind tried to go blank, to deny what she had just heard—to shut out the unbearable pain of his horrific accusations, angry words that stabbed at her heart. Her eyes widened with fear as her fingertips went to her lips. The words tumbled out before she could stop them.

"No…this can't be happening. It's Jerry all over again. I thought you were different, that you really cared about me." A sob caught in her throat. "But you've made it very clear that you don't. You're just like him. I can't go through this heart-breaking turmoil and cruel rejection again."

Tears filled her eyes. Her purse fell from her trembling hand as she whirled around, yanked open the door, and dashed out into the darkness, clutching her car keys in her other hand. He spurned her, just as Jerry had done two years ago. All the hurt, all the fear, it flooded through her, leaving only the horrible pain of betrayal in its wake. Betrayal and a cold fear of what the future held.

Rain pelted her face, tears burned her eyes, and sobs choked in her throat as she ran blindly through the dark toward her car.

Chapter Eleven

A terrifying numbness lodged in the pit of Rance's stomach as he stood in the doorway frozen to the spot, unable to force himself into action. Never in his life had he experienced the type of emotional upheaval gripping him at that exact moment. He watched Darvi's taillights disappear into the rainy night.

He shut the door and sank into the couch as he tried desperately to sort out what had just happened. He sat motionless for what seemed like a long time, his mind clouded with bitter and angry memories. How could Darvi have done this to him? She had actually tried to pull the same scam as his ex-wife, lying to him about being pregnant. The only difference being, unlike Joan, he loved Darvi more than he was able to fully comprehend or explain. He felt empty inside, as if his life had been drained off with nothing left for him.

It must have been a full fifteen minutes before he was physically able to rise from the couch. The fog finally cleared from his mind. The reality of the horrible confrontation that had just happened with Darvi slowly seeped into his consciousness. Joan represented history. That entire nightmare had been ten years ago. He had held on to the emotional baggage far too long. He needed to let go of the negative, to replace it with something positive. Darvi was now, his present and his future, more important to him than anyone. He loved her.

But he had actually stood in the doorway and allowed the woman he loved to drive off into a storm without doing a thing to stop her. Her final words rang loud and clear in his ears, words he hadn't focused on at the time she said them. She had compared him to her former lover, a man who had cruelly betrayed her in her time of need, a despicable act no decent man would do.

Rance closed his eyes and clenched his fists, the moment ripping his insides to shreds. It was the same despicable action he had just inflicted on a woman he loved more than he was capable of expressing.

He forced his body to move as he broke out of his stupor. He raced for the phone and dialed her number. He heard the muffled sound of her ring tone. His gaze landed on her purse where it had fallen on the floor. He picked it up and found her cell phone inside. She was out there in a storm in the middle of the night without any means of communication, no money, and no identification.

The trepidation built inside him as he quickly dressed. He drove straight to Darvi's studio as his anxiety grew more intense. Her car wasn't there. He pounded on the door and rang the bell. No one answered. Full-fledged panic raced through his veins enveloping every corner of his being. He took the key she had given him and entered the studio. He quickly moved through each room, turning on lights, calling her name, but to no avail. Only an eerie silence prevailed, one that seeped into the depths of his growing fears.

He stood at Darvi's front door looking out, trying to peer through the darkness and rain. He ran over all the possibilities, any place she might have gone. A thought clicked in his mind. He grabbed his cell phone and dialed

Amy.

Frank's sleepy voice growled into the phone. "This better be important."

"Sorry, Frank. It's Rance. I need to speak to Amy, and yes, it's very important."

"Sure thing, I'll get her."

A moment later, Amy came on the line. "What is it, Rance? Is something wrong?"

"Is Darvi at your house?"

"Here? No, she's not here. I haven't seen her since we were at the inn earlier today." Concern filled Amy's voice along with a hint of apprehension. "What's wrong?"

"Damn!" He paused as he tried to think. "Where would she go, Amy? Where could she be?"

"I don't understand. Is she missing? What's happened?"

"She came to my house late this evening. When she left she was extremely upset. She drove off in the rain without her purse or cell phone. I can't find her anywhere, and I'm very worried. I'm at her place right now, and she's not here. Your house is closer to mine than her studio. I was hoping maybe she had gone to you to get out of the storm."

"Oh, no. What did you say to her? I know she was very worried. She didn't know how you were going to take the news."

Her words caught him totally by surprise. "What is this, Amy? Does everyone in town know Darvi's pregnant? Am I the only one who didn't know?"

There was a long silence on the other end of the line.

"Amy? Amy, are you still there?"

"Yes, I'm still here, and no, she didn't tell everyone

in town. She didn't even tell me. I guessed it. I don't understand you, Rance. Is that the tone you used with her? Is that the totally unacceptable attitude you dumped on her? No wonder she was so frightened at the prospect of telling you she was pregnant."

Amy's accusations hit him like a hard slap across his face. Darvi had been afraid to tell him? He realized she had been upset about something, but her being afraid to talk to him had never entered his mind.

He took a calming breath. "I'm sorry, Amy. I didn't mean to snap at you like that. It's just that this entire thing came out of nowhere, caught me totally by surprise. I…well, I didn't take the news in a very compassionate or understanding manner." Urgency seized him. "I've got to find her. She can't be out there, wandering around in this storm, alone, frightened, and thinking I've rejected her. Do you have any idea where she might have gone?"

"No." Amy's voice remained distant and cold. "None."

"If she shows up at your place, don't let her leave. Call me on my cell. I'll check with you later."

"Where are you going?"

"I'm going to look for her." Rance disconnected from the call. He leaned forward, resting his elbows on his knees, his head in his hands. A dark fear seeped into his consciousness. He raised his head and opened his eyes as the fear spread through him. He reached for the phone again.

"Sandy Cove Sheriff's Station."

"Sergeant Maxwell and hurry."

Rance bristled. It seemed like hours before the familiar voice came on the line. "Maxwell."

"Tom, it's Rance. I need your help, right away."

"Sure, buddy. What's the problem?"

"It's Darvi. I can't find her. She left my place in…uh, in a very distraught condition. She's out in this storm somewhere. I'm at her house right now, but she didn't go home. Could you check? See if any of your deputies have spotted her car? Maybe she had car trouble somewhere or something…" The possibilities darted through his mind. "She doesn't have her purse with her—no money, no identification, no cell phone."

Tom's voice took on the air of authority that went with his job. "Give me a description of her car. Do you know the license number?"

He provided as much information about her car as he knew.

"Got it. I'll get her license plate number from the state computer. We'll also check the Summitville hospital—" He stopped in the middle of his sentence at the sound of Rance's quick intake of breath.

Tom's voice softened. "That's just routine procedure, Rance. I'm sure she's okay. She's probably someplace safe, warm, and dry, just waiting for the storm to lift so she can go home. Don't worry."

"Yeah, I'm sure you're right." He lacked any enthusiasm for his words. "Thanks, Tom. Call as soon as you hear anything. If you can't get me on my cell phone, leave a message with Amy Sutter."

Rance took a calming breath, rushed out into the rain, and climbed into his truck. He shoved the key into the ignition. He wasn't sure where to look, but he couldn't just sit still and do nothing. He drove slowly down the street, carefully checking each vehicle he came across. He covered every possible route between his house and her studio, checked every parking lot of every store, scoured the road to the main highway and back.

Just north of town he hit his brakes and skidded to a halt on the rain-slickened pavement, gripping the steering wheel so tightly his knuckles turned white. He spotted Darvi's car off the side of the road, halfway in a ditch. His heart pounded with fear. It felt as if it would burst out of his chest at any moment. He leaped from his truck and raced toward the disabled car. The cold, driving rain stung his face as the wind howled in his ears.

"Darvi! Darvi, are you all right? Answer me! Darvi!" The howling wind carried away his desperate cries. He lost his footing in the mud, sliding down the side of the ditch. Tumbling out of control, he landed in a pile of debris and brush.

Clawing his way out of the ditch, he grasped at whatever he could find to help pull himself along. Fabric ripped when his jacket sleeve caught on something. A sharp pain jabbed his left leg. Muddy gravel scraped the side of his face as he again lost his footing and slid back into the ditch. His breath came in hard gasps. The pelting rain stung his skin.

Summoning all his energy and strength, he attempted to climb out of the ditch again. When he reached her car, he grasped the side-view mirror to steady his position. It was the passenger door. He tried to open it but found it locked. He made his way around the car, banging on the windows and hood, calling her name. "Darvi...Darvi. Are you in there?"

Rance yanked open the driver's door. Disappointment shuddered inside him along with despair and fear. The car was empty. He raced back to his truck as fast as conditions allowed, retrieved a flashlight, and began a search of the surrounding area. He looked in all directions but found nothing.

A frantic urgency bordering on full blown panic coursed through his veins. Was she all right? If she was okay, where had she gone? If she had been injured—again, where could she be? The pounding rain soaked his clothes through to his skin, but even the hard driving storm was not able to wash away all the mud from his clothes and shoes.

Bright headlights appeared from around the curve of the road headed toward Rance. A sheriff's patrol car pulled alongside him. Tom Maxwell lowered his window. "Did you find her?"

Rance had to yell to make his words heard above the howl of the wind. "This is her car, but she's not here. I've searched the area as best as I could and didn't find her. Have you heard anything?"

"We've checked the hospital and local doctors. No one answering Darvi's description has shown up. Are you sure this is her car?"

"Positive. In fact, that's my jacket in the back seat."

"She probably caught a ride with someone and is home right now. I'll have my men keep their eyes open, but I'm sure she's okay." Tom glanced down at Rance's leg. "Speaking of doctors and hospitals, you'd better get that leg of yours taken care of. It looks pretty bad. And get some attention for those scrapes on your face."

Rance wrinkled his brow in confusion. "My leg?" He glanced down and for the first time noticed what Tom was talking about. His ripped jeans exposed a nasty gash across his thigh from the second fall into the brush pile. He looked at the ugly scrapes and scratches on his hands, then felt the rough scrapes on his face. He knew he had been injured but hadn't realized the severity. Only his adrenaline surge kept him from folding along with his desperate need to find Darvi, to know she was safe. "No. I've got to find Darvi first. I'm okay."

"Let me know if you locate her, and I'll give you a call if I hear anything." Tom closed his car window and headed down the road.

Rance returned to his truck and drove toward town. As he passed the inn, a glimmer caught the corner of his eye. Visibility was terrible. Had he actually seen something, or had it been a trick of the night and the storm? He made a U-turn and pulled up to the inn's front door, under the protection of the entrance portico.

Yes, he saw it. Through the front windows of the lobby he could make out a faint glow coming from the back storage room. The inn obviously still had power. His heart beat faster. The first stirrings of hope invaded his consciousness. Darvi still had a key to the inn's front door. Even though she had dropped her purse at his house, she obviously had her car keys. And her key to the inn?

The inn was less than half a mile from where he had found her car. If she had been able to walk that distance through the storm, then she had to be okay. He closed his eyes and tried to steady his trepidation.

She had to be okay.

Rance shoved through the front door. It being unlocked was a good sign, an indication that she was inside the inn. A gust of wind whipped in behind him, caught the door, and slammed it shut. He stood still and listened for any sound. He heard only the howling wind and the pounding rain. Nothing else. He moved quickly toward the light, hoping against hope that he would find her safe and well.

He reached out with a trembling hand and pushed the partially closed store room door. He held his breath, afraid to breathe as the door swung wide.

His heart sank, all his hopes dashed, as he stared into the room. The light in the store room shone just bright enough to break the darkness with a faint glimmer reaching to the road. Moving blankets were piled against the far wall. They had been left behind when the furniture had been delivered a couple of days before the open house.

Rance looked again. He blinked, clearing his eyes. His heart beat faster as the full impact of what he saw hit him. The blankets weren't folded, they were bunched in a wet, muddy pile. He stepped into the room. As he cleared the door, a quick intake of breath met his ears. He whirled around. Darvi stood behind the door, holding a fireplace poker at the ready. Fear faded from her eyes, and the frightened look on her face softened as her gaze focused on him.

He grabbed her, pulled her into his arms, and held her close. "Darvi…" He rained what seemed like thousands of kisses over her face and neck. "I've been looking everywhere for you. I was scared to death…finally found your car…"

An enormous sense of relief swept through Darvi the moment she recognized Rance, but it lasted only a fleeting moment. The terrible sting and unbearable pain of his betrayal and rejection surpassed everything else. She struggled in his arms, attempting to free herself from his tight embrace. She shoved her clenched fists against his hard chest as she unleashed her emotional pain and anger. "Let go of me! Just leave me alone. I don't need or want anything from you."

He pinned her arms to her side, preventing her from fighting him. "Stop it! We have to talk."

She continued to struggle, refusing to look at him. "We already had our talk. There's nothing left to say. You made your position perfectly clear. I get it. I don't need to hear it again. Now, get out and leave me alone!"

Rance turned loose of her and stumbled back a step. Her angry words shocked him, defiant words that stung like barbs. He made a frantic search of his mind, desperately trying to remember exactly what he had said to her. He had blurted out something, angry words that had come from his own deeply buried emotional turmoil. The anguish on her face and the hurt in her eyes cut through him like a sharp knife penetrating to the depths of his soul.

He ran his fingers through his wet hair and tried to gather his wits as the chill of his soaked clothes settled over him. He grabbed his cell phone. "I've got to call Tom Maxwell and tell him I found you so he can call off the search." He stared at the phone. "Damn…no signal. It must be the storm. The inn's phones haven't been turned on yet—"

A stab of pain buckled his leg. He grimaced and fell back against the wall. A groan escaped his lips as he slumped to the floor.

Darvi immediately knelt at his side. "Rance, what's wrong?"

"My leg. I didn't feel it until now." He grabbed his left thigh. "I guess I was so intent on finding you that I blocked out the pain." He tried to smile, to make light of the injury. "It seems to be making up for it now."

Darvi saw the bleeding gash. "Rance!" She pulled at

his arm. "Come on, we've got to get you to the doctor. That wound needs to be cleaned, and you need stitches. You'll also need a tetanus shot if you haven't had one lately."

"I'll be okay. Just let me rest for a moment."

"Forget it, buster. We're going to the doctor right now. Where's your car? In front of the door? And I hope it's your truck instead of your car. It's heavier and will have better traction on these wet roads."

"Yeah, it's my truck, and it's in the drive under the portico right by the front door." He looked up at her in amazement. "You don't think I'm going to let anyone other than me drive my truck, do you? You've already run your car into a ditch. I won't have my truck suffer the same fate."

"First of all, I didn't run my car into a ditch. Another car came around the curve too wide and ran me off the road. It was driven by a *man*." She calmed down as she again looked at the nasty wound on his thigh. "You and that precious truck of yours. You don't think for a minute that you're going to be able to handle the gas pedal, brake pedal, and clutch with only one viable leg, do you?" She reached out her hand, snapped her fingers in front of his face, then opened her palm. "Give me the keys."

"I can handle it just fine." Rance rose to his feet, then winced as he tried to put his full weight on the injured leg. He held out his arm as he leaned back against the wall, embarrassment heating his face. "I think you're going to have to give me a hand."

She took in the man leaning against the wall wearing wet, muddy clothes. His face and hands covered with scratches and scrapes, his hair plastered to his head, and a bleeding gash in his thigh. The love she felt for him far outweighed her hurt and anger. The harsh edge disappeared from her voice. "You look like you need someone to take care of you. You're a mess."

He wiped a mud smear from her cheek. "Take a look in the mirror. You're no glamour queen yourself at the moment." His voice softened as the love he felt for her welled inside him. "I don't need *someone* to take care of me—I need *you* to take care of me."

He held her gaze for a long moment. "Don't ever run off from me like that again. When I couldn't find you, I was frantic. I panicked. Tom Maxwell has all his on-duty deputies out searching for you."

A sudden blast of cold wind whipped through the lobby and into the store room. The sound of the howling wind became much louder then quieted again as the lobby door opened and closed. Someone had entered the inn. Rance and Darvi both tensed as he immediately turned toward the door, moved her protectively behind him, and motioned for her to hand him the fireplace poker.

"Hello—sheriff's department. Is anyone in here?"

They each expelled the collective breath they had been holding and emitted a sigh of relief.

Rance poked his head around the storeroom door. "In here."

The deputy walked through the lobby. "Well, I see you found her. Is everyone all right?"

"Yeah, we're fine. Nothing a hot shower and some clean clothes won't fix."

Darvi quickly interrupted. "One of us is fine. The other one is stubbornly refusing to seek medical attention."

The deputy glanced down at Rance's leg, then at

Darvi. "Can you take him, or do you want me to drive him to Doc Bradford's place?"

"Help me get him out to his truck. I can take it from there."

"Hey!" A clearly agitated Rance refused to move. "The two of you are talking about me as if I wasn't even here. *I* can get *me* to *my* truck, and *I* can get *me* to the doctor all by myself. *If* I decide that's what I need to do."

The deputy continued to address his comments directly to Darvi, ignoring Rance. "Sergeant Maxwell told me he'd probably say something like that."

"Yes, he's very pigheaded. Give me a hand."

The deputy stood on one side with Darvi on the other as they helped him across the lobby. Rance continued to insist he could walk on his own.

It was almost daybreak when they left the doctor's office. Once the doctor had cleaned out the mud and splinters from his leg, the wound wasn't as bad as it had originally appeared. It had required only a few stitches. The doctor warned Rance it would be sore for a couple of days, and he should change the dressing regularly. Then the doctor gave him the tetanus shot he kept insisting he didn't need.

The main fury of the storm had subsided, and the wind had died down, but the rain continued. It looked as though it would remain constant throughout the entire day. Darvi drove him home. The atmosphere between them remained strained, Rance trying to maintain upbeat banter while Darvi kept silent refusing to respond to his comments or answer his questions.

When they arrived at his place, she retrieved her purse. He checked the messages on his answering machine. There were four from Amy, two from Tom

Maxwell, one from Frank saying Amy was too upset to make her fifth call, and one from the twenty-four-hour service station on the main highway saying the sheriff's department told them to get Darvi's car out of the ditch, and Rance would pay the tow.

Rance glanced at his answering machine. "I seem to have several phone messages piled up from people who couldn't get through to my cell phone. Why don't you take my truck and go on home so you can clean up? I'll grab a quick shower and join you shortly." She stiffened, her eyes flashing with anger. "Please, Darvi...we have to talk."

"As I said earlier, we've already talked. You said all there is to say. You made your feelings perfectly clear. I don't need to hear it again. There's nothing left to say."

"You're wrong. We have to straighten this out."

She stepped back from him before he could wrap his arms around her. "Your injury has been tended to, and you've been delivered home. As far as you and I are concerned...well, as I said, you made your position perfectly clear." She placed the keys to his truck on the table, then turned toward the door. "I can get home by myself."

He reached for her arm, but she moved out of his grasp and walked out the door—once again disappearing into the rain as he stood there, unable to move.

****

Darvi stepped out of the rose-scented bathwater as she wrapped a large bath towel around her body. She grabbed another towel, rubbed the excess water from the tangled mass of copper-colored hair that was now at least clean. She picked up her hair dryer as she combed out the tangles.

While mechanically working at her hair, her thoughts centered on everything that had happened during the previous twelve hours. She needed to keep her head clear, to crystallize her thoughts, to deal with everything logically rather than emotionally. Her first priority should probably be to move to another town. Sandy Cove was a small community. She could not continue to live and work there without running into Rance on a regular basis. She could not raise her child in such a strained atmosphere, where she and her baby would be subjected to his constant presence and rejection, and where they would be the subject of ongoing local gossip.

She glanced at the clock—eight-thirty in the morning. She had not gotten any sleep the previous night. She needed to call Barney Daniels in Summitville to postpone their meeting, then reschedule her doctor appointment. After that, she had to make a plan for her future, a plan for herself and her baby. Fortunately, George had just paid her for her work on the inn, and he had added an unexpected bonus. It would give her the money to once again make a fresh start somewhere else.

Tears welled in her eyes, and pain stabbed at her heart. A fresh start… That's what she thought she was doing when she left Laguna Beach and tried to put the horrible experience of Jerry Peterson behind her.

Sorrow weighed heavily on her as she expelled a sigh of resignation. Just when she thought she had a bright, sunny future with a man she loved very much, her life suddenly took a drastic turn into the unknown. Her fresh start crashed around her. And now, she had to make a fresh start again.

Somehow, she had to find the strength to make it

happen. Hopefully, this would be the last time.
She reached for the phone.

Chapter Twelve

Darvi awoke with a start, the bath towel still wrapped around her body. Only somehow she ended up underneath the covers with Rance sleeping beside her. The rain continued to pound against the roof and outer walls of the studio.

She remembered stretching out on top of the comforter after she had rescheduled her appointments. She'd intended to rest for just a few moments, then get busy with the many decisions she needed to consider to move on with her life, starting with where to move.

Several hours had passed since then. She had no memory of Rance's arrival, his covering her, and lying down next to her. She gazed at his sleeping face, then tentatively reached over and carefully brushed some errant locks of hair from his forehead. She looked down at the dressing covering the stitches in his thigh. She wanted to cry as she delicately ran her fingers across the scrapes and scratches on his face.

She quietly slipped out of bed and sat in the chair as she watched him. She had been torn about what to do. Should she wake him and tell him to go home? Or, knowing that he had not gotten any more sleep than she had the previous night, let him stay until he woke up on his own, then send him home? A couple of hours passed before he stirred.

He turned over, automatically reaching out for her.

As his weight twisted on his injured leg, he winced in pain and quickly sat up. He looked around as if trying to get his bearings, to connect the previous night's events in his head. His fingers gently pushed at the bandage on his thigh, then ran across his battered cheek and over his chin.

Darvi rose to her feet, determined to take immediate control of the situation before he had a chance to assert his authority in that aggressive way of his. "Well, now that you're awake, you can get dressed and go home. You can also return my front door key. You won't be needing it any longer."

She tried to stop the tremors that rippled through her body, one after the other. She hugged her arms around her shoulders in an effort to ward off the chill that suddenly engulfed her. "You made it very clear that you don't want the baby, that you believe I lied about being pregnant. You also made it clear that you think I'm trying to scam you...trap you into something. Well, my baby and I certainly don't need you or your..." A sob caught in her throat. "Or your accusations."

He grabbed her wrist, then pulled her down on the bed next to him. He twined his fingers in her long hair and nestled her head against his shoulder as he forced her into his embrace. "I'm sorry my words hurt you. I didn't mean for them to."

"What? You said what you felt—cruel, insensitive words—but you're sorry it somehow upset me? You're surprised those horrible words would hurt me?" Total disbelief filled her voice. "You expect me to believe you accused me of actions that terrible, blissfully unaware that your words might not be music to my ears?"

"I didn't accuse you of—"

"The hell you didn't!"

"It's just that you told me you couldn't have children, then you turn up pregnant. I don't understand any of this pregnancy thing. I know we've never really discussed what direction we were going, what the future held, but…" His voice faltered then he finally blurted out, "You're pushing me too much." His voice turned hard again. "I've been through this before, trapped into a marriage that was doomed from the start by a woman telling me she was pregnant when she wasn't."

She pulled free of his arms, her heartache and anger flying through the air toward him. "I'm pushing you? You've been pushing me from the day we met, forcing me to talk about things I didn't want to face. Making me dredge up a horrible time from my past, *the* most emotionally painful thing I've ever experienced." Her voice became almost inaudible. "Until now."

Then her anger flared again. "And you put me through that hell just to satisfy your curiosity about my past?" She stormed across the room, putting some distance between them. "And as for trying to tie you down with some ruse about being pregnant? Only someone as arrogant as you would assume every woman in the world considers you a prime catch!"

She glared at him. "I never once said anything about marriage or even obligations. I don't see why you're so upset. I only said I was pregnant. What makes you assume you're even the father?"

A sob shuddered through her, then she thrust out her chin in defiance. "In fact, you're not the father. So there. I'm officially notifying you that you have no obligation to me or my baby. *My* baby. Not our baby. I'm not holding you responsible, personally or financially. We'll get along just fine without any help from the likes of you. I'll be moving out of town in the next couple of weeks as soon as I locate a new situation for me and *my* baby, which will permanently sever any connection between you and me. You'll be free to continue with your…your selfish life. Only you matter. Only your feelings are valid."

Rance physically recoiled, her words tantamount to a bucket of cold water thrown in his face. What was he doing? Had he temporarily lost his mind?

He took a calming breath in an attempt to clear his thinking. He climbed out of bed, being careful of his leg, then crossed the room to where she stood. He placed his trembling hands on her shoulders.

She may have been putting up a brave front spurred by her anger, but he could see how truly frightened she was. He could see it in the depths of her eyes. At that very second he knew, beyond a shadow of a doubt, that the only thing more terrifying than making a lifetime commitment to Darvi was the thought of losing her forever.

He studied her for a moment. "What do you think you're doing, giving me an out? Letting me off the hook? Of course I'm the father, it's my child. *Our* child."

He drew her to him in spite of her attempt to break free. He kissed her gently on the cheek and whispered in her ear, "It's our child…created from our love." He rocked her in his arms. He no longer feared the words that had lived in his heart. "I love you, Darvi. I love you very much. You don't know how worried I've been about you, knowing something was wrong, but not knowing what. I imagined every terrible thing that could possibly be, but refused to accept any of the possibilities."

Darvi was not sure she had heard him correctly. Could it be? She tried to talk, but couldn't get her voice above a whisper. "Did…did you say love?"

"Yes, I did. I've wanted to tell you for a long time. I think maybe as long ago as the first time we made love." He paused for a moment as if trying to gather the rest of his thoughts. "Just now, when I thought I had actually lost you—literally driven you away from me by putting words to my fears—I realized exactly how much I love you. I'm not afraid to say it anymore. I love you, Darvi. You're my entire life. Without you, my life is empty, nothing but a void without substance."

"You don't know how much I've longed to hear you say those words." She took in a steadying breath, desperately wanting to instill a calm to her voice. "But now, you've made it very difficult for me to believe them. You accuse me of terrible things one minute, then the next you turn around and say you love me. Am I supposed to just accept that at face value? As if nothing happened? Words have meaning, Rance. They carry weight and have consequences. They don't just go away because you say *oops* or *never mind,* then want to take them back. Once those words have been spoken, they can't be erased."

She drew in another deep breath. "You want to take them back, but for how long? Until the next time you're unhappy about something? Those words penetrate into the depths of the soul, and they hurt. What happens tomorrow? And the next day? Will you still be harboring those doubts and resentments? Still thinking I've tried to manipulate you? All your fancy words suddenly professing your love won't change those deeply held feelings of yours then attack me again at the slightest provocation."

She pulled free of his embrace. "I can't live my life that way, each day wondering if you're going to revert to your original beliefs. Each day living in fear of your ultimate rejection and betrayal. I refuse to raise my child in an unsettled atmosphere, one of never being sure where things stand. I want my child to be raised in a home where love truly exists, no matter what obstacles may occur. And if that means raising my child by myself, then that's the way it will be.

"I've been so scared the last few days. I didn't know what you'd think, how you'd take the news. Believe me, I was as surprised by all of this as you are. I didn't purposely mislead you. I sincerely thought I couldn't get pregnant again. I thought I was coming down with the flu. I only went to the doctor to see if he could give me a shot or something, so I'd be okay for the open house. And then when I finally worked up the courage to tell you, instead of support and caring, or even straight forward questions, all I got from you was ugly accusations thrown at me about your belief that I was lying to you, trying to manipulate you the way your ex-wife had. Even after ten years, you're still angry with her, but you're taking it out on me."

"Please...please forgive me." He pulled her back into his arms. "There is no rational excuse for my behavior. In fact, irrational would probably best describe my actions, the angry words I didn't mean. I reacted based on my own painful past, a totally inappropriate response to here and now. All I can do is tell you how very sorry I am, how much I regret my horrible behavior. I promise, with all my heart and soul, I'll spend the rest of my life making it up to you."

"I want to believe you, Rance." A hard tremor shook her body. "I really do. But how can I? Those may be your words now, but they certainly weren't your words or actions last night."

"I love you, Darvi. Nothing is going to change that. All I can do is ask you to please forgive me. I make a solemn promise that I'll spend the rest of my life making it up to you."

She closed her eyes, her inner turmoil playing havoc with her emotions. Did she dare trust the words he had just said rather than his words from last night? These words said with deliberateness and purpose rather than those that were blurted out as a spontaneous utterance? She wanted to believe him. With every fiber of her being, she wanted to believe him, but was she letting her desires overrule the reality of the situation?

Darvi slowly opened her eyes. She saw a wide range of emotions covering his face and in the depths of his eyes. And they all seemed to be saying one thing, that she should believe and forgive. Her heart pounded. Her decisions weren't any longer just about her. She now had another life to take into consideration. Most important was doing what would be best for her child.

Her love for Rance finally made her decision. "I hope I'm not making the biggest mistake of my life." She took a calming breath. "I love you, Rance."

"This isn't a mistake." He brushed a loving kiss against her lips. "This was meant to be. We'll be a family. A happy, loving family."

She snuggled closer to him. "I love you with all my heart—in spite of all your faults." She raised her head and looked intently into his clear blue eyes. "Actually, other than being stubborn, arrogant, pushy, and slightly possessive, you don't have too many faults."

His eyes crinkled with amusement. "Oh, I see. Just those minor ones plus a few insignificant others." He brought his mouth to hers, gently filling her with his caring. His kiss spoke of his unconditional love.

Rance closed his eyes and allowed a smile to curl the corners of his mouth. He kissed her on the forehead. "A baby. We're having a baby. I love you, Darvi Stanton. I love you so much. This is all so incredible."

He shook his head, not knowing what to say or how to behave. He led her over to the edge of the bed, where they sat down.

"We have plans to make, things to talk about. First of all—" He placed his fingertips beneath her chin and lifted her face so he could look into her eyes. "—are you okay? Did the doctor say everything was all right?"

"Yes, everything is fine. I had a follow-up appointment for one o'clock this afternoon, but I rescheduled it this morning when I got home. Now, I go back Wednesday morning at nine o'clock."

"That's why you didn't want me to go to Summitville with you for your meeting with Barney Daniels? Well, I'm going with you to see the doctor on Wednesday." He left her no room for argument or disagreement.

"Oh?" She looked at him with amusement. "You've decided that, have you?"

"Absolutely. That matter is settled. Now, on to the next item. I think we should get married next week. We could be the inn's first honeymooners—"

"Married!" Darvi blurted out the word, no question that what he had just said truly shocked her. "If you think for one minute I want you to marry me simply because I'm pregnant, then you'd better think again. No way am I spending the rest of my life wondering if you married me because you wanted to or only because, *once again*, you felt trapped into doing the *honorable* thing. I don't want you throwing that in my face in the future."

He shook his head "No, I don't feel trapped. There are no more doubts or fears. I want very much for us to be married. It'll be next week." He felt her tension melt away as she nestled against his shoulder.

"See what I mean? Stubborn, pushy, and slightly possessive." She raised her head, and a flicker of anxiety darted through her eyes. "Are you sure, Rance. Really sure?"

"Yes, I'm very sure. I've never been so sure of anything in my entire life." He sat quietly for a moment. "We'll be married. Our love has created a new life— we've produced a child. We'll be a family. It's more than I dared hope for, more than I dreamed could ever be. I'm so very happy." He lowered his head to hers, his lips soft and tender as they met her mouth.

Darvi felt his love as he kissed her. Her head was swimming, her mind in a complete muddle as the magnitude of everything that had happened over the last few days overwhelmed her. Just the night before it seemed as if her entire world had come crashing down around her. And now, she and Rance were going to be married. They were going to be a real family. He was pleased about the baby, wanted the baby. Everything was so perfect, so wonderful.

She put her arms around his neck and returned his kiss and his love. Never in her life had she felt so full of love, joy, and fulfillment as she did at that moment. Her emotions soared. She felt as free to reach the emotional heights as was possible for any human being.

Darvi pulled her mouth away from his, her breathing ragged, matching his. "Rance…"

He recaptured her mouth as his hand slowly untucked the large bath towel wrapped around her body. He dropped it as her hands slid across his bare skin, her fingers ruffling his chest hair.

He laid her back on the bed. Her head rested against the pillow as he gently cupped her breast. He slipped his tongue between her lips.

She eagerly responded to his touch, the sensual stirrings moving quickly through her body. Her tongue danced with his, her foot rubbing seductively against his calf. Her hands caressed his back and shoulders.

His lips moved across her cheek, down her neck to her shoulder. Tingling waves rippled across her skin. A moan of pleasure escaped her lips as he drew her nipple into his mouth, gently sucking, his tongue playing across the pebbled texture.

Darvi lost herself to his electrifying touch, to the heated passion building deep inside her. Never in her life had she believed love could be so marvelous, so full of pleasure, so steeped in the pure joy of living. She loved everything about Rance. The way he physically touched her body and the way he emotionally touched her heart and soul.

He released her puckered nipple from his mouth, kissing the underside of her breast, before moving across her stomach. "Oh, Rance—I love you so much."

His fingertips trailed across her abdomen then ran lightly up her inner thigh. She shuddered as a delicious sensation pulsed through her body. His lips moved across her abdomen, titillating her skin. His fingertips lightly teased the folds of her femininity, heating her taut nerve endings.

They slowly and sensually shared the delights of making love—their bodies and souls totally in sync, their love for each other swirling around them, cloaking them in an overwhelming joy.

He nuzzled her neck as his heated arousal slowly penetrated the moist warmth of her body. She melded with his sensual rhythm. They moved together as one.

"I love you, Darvi." His husky voice held a breathless quality. "I love you so much, you and the baby."

The convulsions shook her body as his words released the incendiary sensations that had been rapidly building inside her. He shuddered as he tightened his hold on her, his release quickly following hers.

The afternoon turned to evening as the rain continued to fall. They floated on a cloud, savoring every intimate moment of their togetherness.

Rance cradled Darvi in his arms as she slept. He watched her, listened to her slow, even breathing. He still had difficulty comprehending the enormity of everything that had happened. He lightly touched his fingertips to her abdomen, marveling at the life they had created, the life growing inside her. He leaned forward and gently kissed her, his lips touching the same place his fingers had just caressed. Then he rested his head against her stomach, wrapping his arms around her hips.

Darvi slowly stirred then opened her eyes. She reached out and brushed his cheek, her fingers touching the scrape marks on his face. She smiled at the wonder on his face and the glow in his eyes. He raised his head, his mouth seeking out hers. He kissed her tenderly, then again rested his cheek against her stomach.

"Darvi, honey, did the doctor say whether it was a boy or a girl?" His voice was soft and loving, the strange mysteries of life imbuing him with a happiness he had never imagined.

She chuckled as she ran her fingers through his tousled hair. "You're ahead of the game. The only tests we did were to determine whether I was pregnant. The rest is yet to come."

He raised his head and looked at her. "Which do you want, a boy or a girl?"

She leaned forward and gently kissed him. "It doesn't make any difference. I'll be happy either way. How about you?"

For a moment, Rance looked pensive. "At first, I wanted a little boy. I think that's natural. All men want a son to carry on the family name, to play ball with"—he grinned—"all that guy stuff." He became thoughtful again. "Then I started thinking about a little girl." He brushed his fingertips across her cheek and tucked an errant tendril of hair behind her ear. "A precious little bundle who would look just like you. A beautiful little girl with emerald green eyes and copper-colored hair."

He sat up, drew her to him, and held her tightly. "You know, Mrs. Coulter—Darvi Anne Coulter—I am the luckiest man on the face of the Earth."

She chuckled. "Mrs. Coulter? Isn't that just a bit premature?"

He grinned at her. "I like the way it sounds. It's perfect."

Epilogue

Darvi stood in the doorway of the workshop and watched as Rance sanded the wood to a satin smooth finish. She could see it in his face, in the way he paid meticulous attention to each and every detail no matter how small. The work was a labor of love.

The two-story doll house stood three feet high, six feet wide, and a foot and a half deep. He had started it two months ago, the day after their daughter had been born. Each and every room was built to scale and had all the details of a real house. There were closets with doors that actually opened and closed, shelves, cabinets, and drawers. There was a wide curving staircase between the floors similar to the one at the inn. As soon as he finished the doll house, he would start on the miniature furniture.

"You know she won't be old enough to play with it for quite a while." Darvi crossed from the door to the work bench, carrying the tiny pink bundle in her arms.

Rance looked up at the sound of her voice, surprised to see her standing there. He had been so absorbed in his work, he had not heard her enter his workshop. A soft chuckle escaped his throat. "It might take me that long to make all the furniture."

He put his tools down, wiped the sawdust from his hands and arms, and smiled at his family. His face radiated his pleasure at seeing them. He brushed a loving kiss against Darvi's lips, then gently touched his fingertip to his daughter's cheek. "Darvi, honey, isn't it time for Jillian to be in bed?"

"I was just about to tuck her in. I thought I'd give you a chance to say good night."

He glanced at his watch. "I think I'll call it a night out here. Give me a moment, and I'll go with you." He cleaned up his work area then washed his arms and hands to make sure all the sawdust had been removed. They went into the house.

"Here, let me." Rance took the baby from Darvi and held her in his arms, his reality filled with wonder and awe as he peered at her tiny face. His words came out as almost a reverential whisper. "She's beautiful, just like you." He carefully placed his daughter in the crib—the crib he had made by hand. "Good night little Jillian. I love you."

He clasped Darvi's hand in his as they left the nursery. They walked down the hallway together to the den and settled onto the couch. Flames danced in the fireplace, throwing soft patterns of light and shadow across the walls. He put his arm around her shoulder and drew her against him. "I love you, Mrs. Coulter." He leaned over and placed a soft kiss on her lips. "I love you very much."

"I love you, too, Mr. Coulter."

They sat in silence, basking in the deep love that filled the house.

A word about the author...

USA Today Bestselling Author Shawa Delacorte lived most of her life in Los Angeles and earned a living for twenty years by working in television production. She was always interested in writing and dabbled at it but not seriously. She combined her interest in writing with her avocation of photography and began doing magazine articles featuring her photographs. After selling several articles, she discovered she enjoyed the writing process as much as the photography.

Shawna's friends told her that she should make use of her television contacts and write scripts. She enrolled in a screen writing class at UCLA. By the close of class she knew screen writing was not for her. The other thing she knew was that she wanted to write novels rather than magazine articles.

~*~

Visit Shawna at
www.shawnadelacorte.com
https://shawnadelacorte.blogspot.com